Confessions of a girl with a wanderlust

Confessions of a girl with a wanderlust

too hot to handle
— sizzling diaries of
desire and discovery

Angelina King

PAVILION

This edition published in the United Kingdom in 2013
First published in the United Kingdom in 2007 by
Pavilion Books
10 Southcombe Street
London W14 0RA

An imprint of Anova Books Company Ltd

ISBN 978-1-909108-54-7

A CIP catalogue record for this book is available from the British Library.

10 9 8 7 6 5 4 3 2 1

Reproduction by Rival Colour Ltd, United Kingdom
Printed and bound by 1010 Printing International Ltd, China.

www.anovabooks.com

CONTENTS

PROLOGUE

It started out a day like any other. Out of the door at eight; tumble on to the tube; pick up a huge frothy coffee and an irresistibly sticky pastry and at my desk by half past. Ease myself into the day by checking my messages and reading the gossip mailings, then down to work.

Except that day I stopped ten paces into my office and read the note stuck to my computer screen.

'Go home. Get your passport and your toothbrush and get yourself to Heathrow. I'll call you at 11. Paulo.'

Tessa, the office manager, appeared by my side. 'He left first thing this morning. He's on a plane himself now, but by the time you get to the airport he'll be able to give you a call about joining him.'

'Joining him where?'

'He forgot to mention. I have a feeling Paris, but I'm not sure. I think he just wants someone to help him make the presentation this afternoon. Go on, you'll have to hurry if you want to get there by eleven . . .'

Just over two hours later I was sitting with my second coffee of the day waiting for my mobile to ring. I felt oddly nervous and excited. It wasn't the first time I'd had to travel on business – I'd been working for the fashion label MV for over a year now, first as a shop assistant and then within three months as a window dresser for the London stores, and I'd had to go to Rome the previous autumn on a training course. Most of my friends were still at college, but I'd skipped a gap year and finished a year before them, so while they were still hunched over essays and overdraft letters, I was spending my time (and money!) collecting cocktails, high heels and all the glossy design books and magazines I hadn't been able to afford before. Rome had been brilliant, and though I tried not to boast to my friends, it had been thrilling to scoot off for those three days; to see the buildings I'd read about; visit glamorous bars and restaurants and enjoy looking at beautiful Italian boys. Oh, and learn how to do my job.

I liked window dressing, even though my dad was perplexed by my first career move. All I'd ever been good at was art, but working was nothing like college; MV valued my creativity, but I had to focus it on a very specialist area and tailor it to an idea of taste. Still, that was enjoyable, and I gave free rein to my own creative obsessions and ideas in my spare time, photographing whenever I could. Since Johnny and I had split up, I'd had more free hours than before, and I tried to put them to good use, rather than brooding. I missed him, though; missed him a lot, actually.

My mobile rang and I snapped to attention, Johnny banished from my mind. 'Paulo?'

'Eleanor, hi. You're there, I hope?'

'Heathrow, yep. Paulo –'

'Good girl,' he interrupted. 'Sorry about the short notice. I've got them to reserve you a place on the next plane to Paris. You'll be here by lunchtime – get a cab to L'Atelier and I'll meet you there. OK?'

'OK,' I said, and scribbled down the flight details.

'We'll be staying in the Chanson as well tonight – I said we'd go to a breakfast meeting with the team here tomorrow before we leave. Hope you've brought a pair of clean knickers with you.'

Paulo laughed at his own comment, then rang off. I shook my head; I wasn't offended. My boss was always trying to embarrass me, and reminded me constantly how ridiculously young he considered me. 'I'm not taking advice from someone younger than my car,' he'd say if I made suggestions, but he was a good, fair manager and I'd already learned so much from him in the time I'd been with the company.

Besides, despite his age and his bad jokes, he was a good-looking man and I usually enjoyed myself around him. He wore black glasses and a suit every day, and though I teased him for looking overly 'Media', he didn't mind, probably because he knew he looked good. There were both male and female staff in the company who'd watch him for a second too long as he walked through the store in Bond Street, myself included.

CHAPTER 1

PARIS

I arrived in Paris feeling great. No thanks to the flight, I should say, but there is something about airports and travelling alone – at a civilized hour – that makes me feel sophisticated: like the woman I didn't dare dream I'd become back in the sixth form. I'd barely had any time to change for the trip and the afternoon's meeting, but thankfully my months at MV had taught me the knack of dressing elegantly in five minutes flat. I'd torn off that day's window-dressing uniform of jeans and white T-shirt, and thrown on a black wrap dress, some shiny high heels, red lipstick and a cute black beret I'd been waiting for an opportunity to wear.

The plane touched down and, in no time it seemed, I jumped in a cab and touched up my make-up, and as I did so I remember I felt full of myself, excited that Paulo had chosen me to go out for the meeting over the other juniors. The driver looked at me now and again in his rear-view mirror, but he didn't say a word, concentrating largely on weaving through the streets at a great pace, and I looked out and loved what I saw. The city looked beautiful in the spring sunshine, the men and women becoming more elegant and attractive as we drew towards my destination. We pulled up at L'Atelier, an ancient-looking pavement café, and I paid the driver and skipped towards Paulo, who was waiting at the end table. He stood to kiss me.

'How are you, kid?' he asked, grinning at me, teasing me for my evident enthusiasm. 'Thanks for coming out so sharpish. Not that you had a choice.'

I decided not to take the bait. Paulo was not interested in small talk, and as soon as he'd given me a chance to order a coffee he leaned over and said, 'Good news, shopgirl. I've decided to promote you.'

I looked at him, perplexed.

'You can be the Assistant Merchandiser. Proper role. Not just an add-on to your job any more. Starting now.'

'Are you serious?' I asked.

'Don't question me! Do you want it or not?'

I nodded dumbly, a wide smile spreading across my face.

'Great. Starting now, like I said. We'll train you, of course. You've done a brilliant job back in London – you're good with people, and you've got a fantastic eye. That's a rare combination. You'll need to go to as many of the branches as we can fly you to this season and next, pick up the whole MV philosophy across the major cities, and then by next year you'll be an absolute asset to us. Instead of a liability.'

This time I was just too shocked to notice, let alone rise to, the insult. I'd thought it might take two or even three years to get a true break in merchandising for a company like MV. Now it was all unfolding easily in this instant, in this café, in this loveliest of settings. It felt too good to be true, but I knew that Paulo wouldn't mess around. As I watched him over the top of my coffee, he outlined what would be required of me: which stores in which cities I would need to visit, the people I would work with and learn from; the 'networking' I would need to do – 'That means staying sober at evening functions, not necking four champagnes and copping off with some bloke from the stockroom, Eleanor' – and how this would equip me for a long career in the industry. As I got into my stride, he said, I would help to develop future seasons' themes, looks and branding. It felt better than my graduation, better than anything I had achieved up to this point. Paulo believed in me, and my confidence soared. I promised myself then that I would make sure his faith in me was rewarded. Later that night, when the news had started to sink in, I had cause to think about some other – more personal – ambitions, too.

In my hotel room, I prepared for the night ahead. The afternoon had gone smoothly, and the team had seemed genuinely impressed with some of the ways we were doing things back in London. Paulo's ideas went down well, and since some of the most senior members of the company were based at the Paris HQ, he was on a high by the end of the afternoon. He'd sent a bottle of champagne to my room and I was enjoying my second glass, still elated by my promotion and dancing around my room, helped by the thoughtfully provided CD player.

I took my time over my make-up, running through the events of the day in my mind. I'd only met one of the French staff before – Estelle – when she'd come over for training the previous year. A good few years older than me, we'd nonetheless gone out and had a great time at a nightclub in King's Cross after work. Now she wanted to show Paulo and I some of the *boites* in the Parisian red-light district in return. We were meeting Estelle and some of the other MV staff in a bar in Pigalle at ten.

When I think back to that night, especially early on that night, I feel a kind of affection for my old self. I was so happy about my new job that I had not begun to really think how the coming months would change me. I would be travelling, alone, in foreign cities, for days at a time. I would be staying in some great hotels, meeting new people every time and having to work and socialize with them until it no longer held any fear for me. I would be by myself and responsible for myself. Above all, although I did not yet know it,

I would learn just what I was capable of, and how to please myself.

After supper the seven of us just weren't ready to go home. Estelle suggested to her colleagues that we visit another nearby bar. This was a special one, she promised: Paris style, for the tourists. I blithely followed the little crowd through a contented fug induced by good food and delicious wine, not noticing Paulo's amused smile and look of anticipation.

The door to the bar was set back from the street. It was clear that you needed to know about it in advance to find this place; no one would just stumble in unwittingly. The door was dark and high and solid looking, with a polished silver fox knocker. Estelle raised this and slammed it three times against the thick wood, and a small, pretty blonde woman immediately opened the door.

Inside, the air was thick with fragrance and chatter. Low murmurings echoed around the oddly darkened room. We headed straight to the bar and ordered a round of long vodka and elderflower cocktails, cool-tasting and powerful. As the other women removed their coats, and the men began to look around, I noticed something odd about the other punters. No, punters was the wrong word. These people made up that most old-fashioned of things: a clientele. The men looked to me as though they were from another era. Without exception they were elegantly dressed in dark trousers, crisply tailored shirts and proper shoes; not a sneaker in sight. Normally I would have assumed men so well turned out to be gay and thought no more of it, but there were no male couples or groups here. Instead, each man sat with a woman, talking earnestly and attentively to her and, I noticed, sometimes even listening! I turned in delight to one of the MV employees and mentioned that it was like walking into the set of an old-school date movie, and she laughed hard.

After a second drink at the bar, I began to see why. Kissing in bars in London often led to cheerful jeers of 'Get a room!' and was generally considered sweet but naff. Here, especially as the night drew on, kissing was open and determined. On my way to the bathroom, I noticed a couple talking intimately at the far end of the bar. She sat on one of the high stools, long legs showing through side slits in her skirt, luxuriant red curls spread out over her shoulders. I was tipsy and she was so beautiful, her hair so glamorous and different to the usual head of highlighted, blonde, straightened hair girls in bars wore at home, that I stopped to stare. As I did so, the man stopped talking and began kissing the woman hard on the mouth and neck. My immediate instinct was to drop my gaze and look away, but I realized that although all his physical attention was directed at his date, the man's eyes were on me. We stood in an odd triangle, the woman's eyes shut as they kissed, his open, and he did not look away from me. It was then that I noticed a movement, and realized with a lurch of embarrassment that his hand was not on the woman's thigh as I had assumed, but inside her skirt, moving delicately but unmistakably to and fro, and her thighs were parted, not widely but enough, and now I had seen this I realized that her eyes were not just closed for the kisses.

I could feel my cheeks were already burning. They were so shameless! I was embarrassed and confused. Hadn't anyone else seen what I had? Wouldn't they get thrown out? I wanted to tell my colleagues what I had witnessed so we could giggle and make light of it, but on the other hand I didn't want them to laugh at my shock. It wasn't the first time I'd seen people being amorous in clubs or bars, of course. It wasn't even that I had never been amorous in a club or bar myself! It was more the brazen look on the man's face: almost an invitation. Although the movement I had seen was tiny, the eye contact had unsettled me, and what I imagined happening beneath the flimsy cover of the skirt disturbed me further still, because I could feel myself getting turned on, almost as much as if it were me being touched like that. I wanted to move away but felt rooted to the spot. My little group was the other side of the bar, and I knew I was out of sight to them, but I worried that one of them would walk round and catch me staring at this poor couple, affording them no privacy, even though I understood (despite myself) that they wanted no such thing.

I think we stood in this little triangle only for a few minutes. I looked on as the man nuzzled into the redhead's neck, and heard him say something in low tones which made her smile without opening her eyes. She shifted on the stool, and I felt myself grow wet as I watched her adjust her skirt discreetly and open her legs just a little further so I could clearly see her pussy, bare and pink and glossy with her own juices, and his fingers sliding slowly, lazily, up and down and over, so that she moved her bottom towards him just a little with every move. I realized my lips were open and my breathing was growing harder, and I looked for I don't know how many seconds and then turned and walked fast and blind into the bathroom. I slid my knickers over my thighs with indecent haste and opened my legs, slipping fingers easily and quickly between them and inside myself, relief and pleasure flooding through me as my breathing came harder still. With my own eyes closed, the imprint on them of the couple was as vivid as if I had still been there in front of them. I reached down further and pushed another finger inside my pussy, hungry and impatient, and slipped my thumb over my clit the way I had watched the man do to his date. I tried to keep quiet but the image was strong in my head: her cunt, his hand, the slipperiness of her, the look on his face, the look on hers with her head thrown back and her thighs open, and I came as silently as I could, my heart pounding and my mind full of what I had seen.

Back at our little corner of the bar, I brushed off my long absence, explaining to the others that I'd had to get a glass of water as the vodka had gone straight to my head. Perhaps it had. I didn't mind the teasing that resulted, not daring to think about what had just happened and how utterly embarrassing it would have been had I been caught staring, or racing to the ladies.

Then Estelle asked me casually if I knew what sort of a bar we were in.

'What do you mean?' I asked.

'Haven't you heard of these? Sex bars. There are lots of them coming up in Paris now. I think some have always been here, but others are quite new. I'm sorry . . .' – she had noticed my cheeks blushing again – 'we didn't mean to embarrass you! Little Eleanor,' and she smiled at me, not unaffectionately. I admitted I had never heard of them.

'Come on, El,' interrupted Paulo. 'You're not such a little innocent, are you?'

His eyes were dark in the dim light, too dark to read, and I could not tell what he was really thinking.

For a horrible moment I wondered if he had brought me to Paris, to this club for that matter, for private motives. The excitement of my promotion and my new job came back to me and I realized again just how much it meant to me, and how heartbroken I would be if it turned out that he saw me simply as a young girl to impress and screw. But another look at Paulo's laughing mouth reminded me of his two main pleasures in life – work and teasing. I knew him well: attractive and charming as he was, he could choose any woman he liked if he wanted sex, and his career was too important to him to jeopardize with messy work flings. I breathed a sigh of relief to myself, and tried to ignore a smaller inner voice – a hint of disappointment beneath that relief.

Virginie, one of the other French staff, turned to me before I could worry about this new, niggling thought. 'Eleanor. You must have seen that the couples all around are not all talking so sweetly to one another, no? Take a peep,' and she made a small gesture with her hand to make me look into the corners of the room, to notice for the first time the booths, the small doors off the main bar leading to who knew what secret areas. I felt so naïve as I saw plainly now that every couple was physically engrossed in one another; where I had seen only intimacy and conversation, it was now clear that the men and women dotted around the room were in various stages of foreplay. The top of one woman's dress was undone to the waist and I could see her nipples in the dim light; even as I watched, her partner bent to take one in his mouth. At another booth I could see three figures. Two men were stroking a woman's arms and hair lovingly, leisurely; one of the men had a strange expression, explained away when I saw a woman's head rise from his lap and realized she had been under the table all along.

There was nothing to say. I laughed ruefully, caught out: the new girl at school, gently made to look foolish and young. It could have been worse. The others explained that they were tourists, they had brought me here simply to show me another side to Paris, and I did not know whether to believe this or not, but we moved on shortly after to a more straightforward bar in the district. Apart from being unable to drop the subject entirely – 'Your face, Eleanor, when you saw that woman come up from his lap!' – my colleagues concentrated on more cocktails and even a little bit of shoptalk. Paulo and I grabbed a cab in the early hours and I fell into bed and a blissful sleep, dreaming of strange dark corners and tall men until, too soon, my alarm clock sounded to rouse me for the breakfast meeting.

CHAPTER 2

BERLIN

When I had awoken in that room in the Chanson in Paris, memories of the night before (as well as an overwhelming hangover!) had come rushing into my consciousness. I felt embarrassed, but it did not detract from the thrill of my career news. I felt that my star, such as it was, was truly in the ascendant.

I thought, too, about the couples we had seen in the bar. In the cool morning light, the early sun throwing blue shadows on the clean white walls of the hotel room, the musk and dark and atmosphere of sex I recalled from the night before seemed unreal. But then I thought of the expression on the men's faces – the one who watched me as he kissed and touched his girlfriend; the one who sat so dazed in the booth as a woman licked or touched him beneath the table – and the instant feeling of arousal it gave me made it seem suddenly very real again.

I wondered about why the night had had such an impact on me. It wasn't, as Paulo had accused me, that I was an 'innocent'. I had slept with several men in my life already, two of whom I had been in love with, the other four – five? – frankly, for fun. Two were friends already, and what with wine, film, low lights and too much chatter, these things would somehow develop. It was lovely to see a different side to a man; to learn how someone liked to be touched; surprising ways they knew of touching you. It was good to lose yourself in the act, to shock yourself, even, at things you might try or enjoy in the heat of the moment.

And yet, had I ever truly done just that – lost myself, let go? Even with Johnny, who had known me more closely than anyone ever had before? Had I really lost myself to our lovemaking, or had I perhaps remained conscious of myself as being separate? Worse, had I thought too much about how I looked or sounded instead of what I felt, even in our most private moments? I knew that I had never felt what the redhead in the bar had seemed to experience: an utter abandonment to pleasure, even in public, to the man's busy hands and mouth, heightened perhaps rather than compromised by my presence. I saw all of this with a clarity I had never known before. To answer my own major question: no, I had not truly let go in the past. I was not getting from sex all that perhaps I could. The thought had never occurred to me before. I came, usually; I had not been unlucky enough to sleep with any man who didn't care about my pleasure. I was experimental, I thought, and mostly when I had slept with someone with whom there was a real connection; if I was lucky that connection could be amazing, and not necessarily in relation to how well I knew or liked the guy! But the previous night had unsettled me. I felt I was missing out on something, without knowing exactly how or what.

So later that week, when Paulo gave me my schedule for the coming months, stretching ahead through the spring to the summer and late autumn, I made a private promise to myself. The new responsibility and reward at work was beginning to sink in properly, so that I could think about and plan how to get the most from the opportunity I'd been given. But as much as I was thrilled and excited about my new job, I would also go about fulfilling some more personal ambitions.

Until that point, I had always been surrounded by people. That sounds a little odd, and it had always been the way I'd wanted things: even at college, when I had loved doing my art degree and the creativity it demanded of me, I was never the kind of student who was completely and exclusively absorbed in the work. The next night out, the next date, was always important to me. I loved the buzziness of that lifestyle. There was always someone around to have coffee with, to work on a shoot with, to go dancing with. There was Johnny, too, keen to spend as much time with me at college as he could, eager to leave his City job behind him. I had, I knew, rarely been left to my own devices.

Now all that was to change. I would be spending a lot of time in my own company – travelling and preparing for meetings – but also in the company of strangers. It was up to me to make an impression, or else sink into the background, whether at work or on the road, at airports and hotels. The people I met would have no preconceived idea of me, and I would be totally out of context: no one would be around to tell new people what I was *really* like! The idea was completely liberating. More than this, it was an idea that worked alongside fantasies I could then barely begin to articulate, even to myself.

I had been with Johnny more or less throughout college, and while I had loved him, I had been relieved in a way when we split up six months earlier. There was a sense of opportunity opening up: I had grown cosy quickly in the relationship, and had missed out on lots of college rituals and deeper friendships as a result – and turned a blind eye to lots of cute boys! I suppose I wanted to make up for lost time, but the weeks since we split had not really seen that happen, so I missed Johnny badly but – I suspected – for the wrong reasons.

The coming months glittered before me now, a vast ocean of unknowns, of chance and adventure. I wanted to explore anonymous cities and hotels, and at the same time explore parts of myself I never had before. I would be a true unknown everywhere I went, and I wanted to try out different identities and fantasies before I lost my nerve.

That was then. I looked down now over the scudding clouds and the dawn sky, strapped in tightly as the stewardess announced we were minutes away from landing at Berlin airport.

Berlin was different. Younger than I had expected, somehow. People were energetic, and this included the staff at the great glass branch of MV in the fanciest part of the city centre. Pushing through the doors on to the shop floor that morning, I was taken aback by the luxurious feel of the store. Of course, all the branches tried to maintain the same levels of plushness; the whole success of the company was based on the way you were made to feel on entering one of the stores. An MV customer was supposed to feel cosseted, happier about life, excited about the atmosphere and lulled into a sense of belonging and entitlement. That last one was important. It was key that customers felt that these products were, in a sense, theirs already: they merely had to select them and spend a moment at the till before they could take their things home. It was hard to explain, and deeply psychological, but if you got it right, you were not so much selling or merchandising as just making it easy for the customer to come in and collect their goods. In this store particularly, just being there, surrounded by glass and sunshine and the smell of fine leather, made you feel very good about yourself indeed.

'Can I help you, Madam?' enquired a polite and very smiley young man of about 23. He was tall with shiny hair and good teeth; the ideal MV salesman.

I explained that I had come from London – 'I work for MV, under Paulo? He told me to ask for Suki.'

'You're Eleanor, then. I am Thörsten. Welcome to Berlin!' More pearly teeth. 'I'll take you to meet Suki now. She'll be delighted you're here.'

Thörsten turned out to be older and more senior than I had assumed. Suki and he and I spent the morning going over the week's notes, covering everything from the current windows to the layout of the interiors section. It was spring outside, and MV was encouraging customers to think about changing their home style, much as they would their wardrobes, to reflect the coming season. There were gorgeous sprigged materials and drapes for the garden, vintage-style tea sets and linen cloths everywhere, suggesting the relaxed kind of luxury that costs a lot of money to create. We looked at spreadsheets and balance sheets and figures and statistics until my head swam. I took notes and worked into the afternoon making sense of all the information I had been given. Late in the day, Thörsten came to find me at one of the upstairs desks.

'Cup of coffee?' he asked, setting a mug down beside me and pulling up a chair. 'You must be just about done here for today?'

'Thanks. Yeah . . . I was thinking I might go and check out the competition later on.' I wanted to visit the other luxury stores in the neighbourhood, see how the other shops looked and felt, as I knew this would be the first thing Paulo would ask me about on my return.

'Well, don't tire yourself out,' said Thörsten. 'I was thinking, you might want a guide to Berlin later. Some of us were going out after work anyway . . .' He trailed off with a sheepish smile and I realized he was half asking me out for work, half for pleasure. I smiled back and accepted his offer, and two hours later a handful of us were settled into a comfortable corner of a bar, a completely white box upholstered everywhere in squashy white leather and lit in various, changing colours. The effect was oddly charming.

We were in about the third bar of the night when I saw him. I was faltering already, having been out since six that morning when I had left for the airport in London. I had intended to come out with my colleagues to experience a taste of the night-time atmosphere of Berlin, before getting a good night's sleep so I could be fresh for a full day and a company dinner the next evening. It never works like that, I know – the nights when you absolutely can't stay out, can't have another vodka and definitely can't go on to a nightclub are the nights when you end up doing exactly that. But I was ready to go back to my hotel room, warmed and sleepy with apple schnapps, despite the energy of the young crowds in the bars.

He came towards me holding a drink, and turned his head to shout something over to a friend just as I took a side step in the wrong direction to avoid him. There was a flurry of ice cubes and apologies, and then we smiled and exchanged names. 'Markus,' he told me. He was a graphic designer who worked for one of the style magazines based in the city; he knew MV well although he couldn't afford to shop there, he said.

Markus had beautiful green eyes behind lovely silver-framed glasses. I had no idea how old he was. I had felt this sort of click with people before: you like the way they look and sound, but you drift away from them and that is that. Tonight I felt no need to drift away from Markus. I thought of my hotel room, and felt a shift inside my head, excitement beginning to build. I felt, let's face it, like a man. The more Markus asked about me – and the more I learned about him – the more I began to wonder if all this was necessary. Or even desirable. I saw it suddenly for what it was: a courting ritual in miniature, a conversation that could also be a precursor for something else, if I wanted it to be. Paulo always said that men would never chat to women for the sake of it. If a man was talking to you, and looking at you with interest, that was all the sign you needed. It was your decision whether to go with it, but in simply standing and talking to you, and asking the odd question, this was the unspoken male come-on: 'I am here, if you want me, and you must dictate the pace.'

I decided to dictate the pace.

In the cab, we didn't bother speaking any more. Markus had clearly dumped his friend in the uncomplicated way men have, and I wasn't interested in how and where Markus had to go later on, or tomorrow. I had kissed, but never before fucked, a man I didn't know at all, and was nervous as well as excited. But then again, I felt good around this guy, and the hotel would be safe, and I tried to forget myself and enjoy the moment. Markus kissed me all the way to the Plaza by the river Spree, and I let him, and it was lovely to let this clean-smelling man hold and kiss me so closely that I could feel his hard on through his jeans.

Inside my room, Markus wondered at the fluffy white towels and robes. 'You lucky girl!' he said in his thick accent. 'Now I can see why you wanted to make the most of this room!'

I threw a towel at him for his cheekiness and he reached over and scooped me on to the bed, holding me tightly and breathing hard again. His body felt tight and strong and warm against my own. We kissed like that for a long time, and he stroked my hair and I thought about the fact that he was growing harder and harder against me. I reached down and squeezed the front of his jeans, and Markus groaned.

'Enough,' he said then. 'Let me see you.'

I rolled away and he motioned for me to stand up. He kneeled on the bed before me, and began to undo my shirt buttons, slipping off the sleeves to reveal my bra properly, running his hands immediately over my breasts and catching his breath – as I did – as my nipples pushed eagerly into his palms. He looked lovely in the too-bright light of my hotel room, still in his shirt and glasses. I began to unbutton his top, and soon we were rolling back on to the bed, clothes disappearing, and skin touching and sliding against skin. I closed my eyes and breathed in his citrussy scent of soap and aftershave and maleness. I felt his hands close firmly around my bottom and opened my eyes abruptly as he slid fingers inside my knickers and then into my already wet pussy. 'Sorry,' he said, 'I couldn't wait. She's lovely.' He pulled himself down the bed and I gasped with pleasure as I felt warm breath, quickly followed by his hot tongue pressing between my thighs. His hands cupped my bottom and he thrust his tongue deep into me, pulling out to swirl it over my clit again. I felt my pussy begin to throb, my bare nipples cold and hard, and I ran my hand down the length of my own body, shuddering as my breasts responded to my own touch. With my eyes closed I forgot where I was and surrendered to the experience, enjoying the contrast between the cold sheet and air of the room and the warmth of his body and tongue; the silky pressure between my legs and all of our hands roaming my body. He rolled one of my nipples gently between his fingers and darted his tongue again and again over my clit and I couldn't help myself; I began to buck and throb and come in his mouth in deep, delicious waves, unaware of anything but a pure, blissful feeling rolling over me again and again. I heard myself moaning and looked up to see him smiling over me, pleased as punch with himself. 'My turn,' he said, and climbed close enough so that I could turn my head and lick the tip of his cock, getting up on to my elbows and taking in more as I got used to the feel and taste of him. He groaned aloud and took my head in his hands, holding me firm as I sucked and licked, and almost without warning I felt him begin to shudder now, and I kept him tight in my mouth as he thrust towards me, his hands in my hair and on my breasts as he pulled me closer and closer as he came.

In the half-light of the morning we finally made love. I awoke to feel his erection pressing between my thighs from behind me, and I twisted away to reach for a condom. I opened my legs and let him push his way inside, cupping my breasts in his palms and then rolling me on to my front to fuck me more firmly. I squirmed to try to increase the pressure on my clit, feeling his breath grow faster and more excited as his thrusts became almost uncomfortably hard. I pushed back hard and brought myself up on to my knees, forcing him up too, so that I was on all fours now, and he fucked me on his knees with a palm on my back, his cock big enough to make me feel stretched and full; I leaned down to feel the full force of it, excited by the pressure. 'Touch me,' I said, and the relief as he rolled his wet fingertips over my swollen, slippery cunt was indescribable. I let my breasts graze against the cover beneath me and concentrated on the rudeness of the position, the submissiveness of it, and the feeling of his hand working between my spread legs, and as I began to come I heard him moan too, his thrusts hard now and almost too much, and we sweated and I cried out and was still, and when I next awoke he had gone.

I lay there for over an hour, replaying the events of the night before in my head. It was unsettling that he had entered and exited my bed – my life, in fact – so abruptly. Would that be it now? We had exchanged no phone numbers, no email addresses; a clean, one-off encounter. It seemed right, but also cold. Usually if something was pleasurable, I would want to repeat it. But neither Markus nor I had made any attempt to make that likely, or even possible. Yet I could still feel him on me; I ached from our fucking; I could smell his aftershave, his sweat, on my skin. He had left an imprint on me, however casually I tried to feel about what happened. I could not say that I missed him, or would miss him: I barely knew him. We met, and were intimate, and now in all likelihood we would never meet again. I dressed for work silently, thinking, remembering, thinking, replaying.

CHAPTER 3

BARCELONA

As a child, Spain meant simple pleasures to me: playing on the sand; swimming in the sea; ice cream and fizzy drinks; making new friends. Really, now that I am in my twenties, and even though I love the glamour of Barcelona, the pleasures Spain holds for me are not so very different to then; I've just added a few more ways of enjoying it.

The flight from London to Barcelona was blissfully short. I had time to think about the work I was supposed to do there, and to flick through a few Spanish fashion and design magazines, but not enough time to get restless. It was only my second trip away alone, and I was keen to make a good impression. Paulo had told me that the flagship branch in Barcelona was run by a slightly scary woman called Rosa. She was keen to meet me; she had mentioned to Paulo that my trip was good timing, as she was suffering from high staff turnover. Rosa wanted someone who knew the company well to create a new layout for the shop floor and windows for the next season's collections, and to teach and collaborate with the new workers. Naturally I was nervous: it was true that I had been with the company for a while now, and the work I had done in visual merchandising had been of a high enough standard to get me noticed, get me promoted – and sent on this trip, in fact. And Paulo had said I had good people skills. But still, I felt a little intimidated by the idea of flying in and bossing around a group of people, some of whom were bound to be older than me.

But it wasn't like that at all. I had built Rosa up into such a dragon in my head that when I finally met her, I was relieved to find her professional and friendly. We spent the morning going through her choices for the shop from the coming collection, and from that afternoon she gave me an office overlooking the harbour to draw up my display plans. I was thrilled, and sat in my slightly uncomfortable black leather sculptured chair feeling very pleased with myself indeed.

I worked hard, stopping only for a couple of the eye-wateringly strong coffees everyone in the building seemed to drink. There was no siesta-time at MV in Barcelona, although from our office I could hear the telltale slamming and banging noises that meant metal shutters were being drawn down for the afternoon across the entrances of hundreds of small shops across the city. By seven o'clock, when the staff finally started leaving, I was exhausted.

'Thank you for today,' said Rosa, popping her head around the door as I packed up. 'I hope they've found you somewhere nice to rest your head?'

'Yes, yes, thank you,' I replied. I didn't want to say too much – Paulo had whispered to me before I left that his assistant had managed to book me into the city's most exclusive hotel on a good rate, and I knew that when Rosa had come to London for a couple of days last year we had stuck her in a nondescript business hotel in Kensington, much to her disgust. Perhaps this was the reason Paulo had found her difficult!

As I left the building, glass doors swinging behind me, I changed my mind about grabbing a cab and decided to walk the few blocks to the hotel. It was a beautiful evening; unseasonably warm for a girl used to British springtime. As I approached the hotel, I looked up and was amazed by its height and its striking modernist design. I had been to Barcelona once before, very briefly, and stayed in a charming but dingy room tucked away at the top of one of the ancient buildings in the Old Town. This was something different entirely: new, but not without character, the curves and swooping glass did not look out of place in a city dotted with Gaudi's imaginative lines and colours. Fading sunlight bounced from the roof back at the sea, illuminating the high top of the building and making it shimmer in a slightly unreal way. I walked into the lobby, grinning at my luck, and checked in.

My room was stark but lovely – a sparkling white space, with plush carpet and a bare marble bathroom. On the way up in the lift, I'd seen photographs of the rooftop bar and pool and I'd promised myself I wouldn't collapse into sleep as soon as I got to my room – I'd throw my bags on the bed, grab my costume and make the most of the evening sun. Within twenty minutes, I was relaxing on a lounger, wearing a silky hotel wrap over my new red polka-dot bikini and clutching an outlandish cocktail, dark glasses on so I could discreetly check out the other guests.

I didn't have much experience of five-star Continental hotels, but I could see what I assumed was a fairly typical mix of guests: Eurotrash women of indeterminate age, anywhere from 25 to 55, wearing gold and big hair; slim, taut gay men in small trunks and little T-shirts, and older men with greying or white hair, too-tanned floppy skin and designer-label flip-flops. I was fascinated. And then there was a handful of people – couples mainly – who just looked good. Wealthy and relaxed and attractive, like the people we liked to depict in our MV lifestyle ads. Luis was one of these people.

I had been looking at a man and woman in their thirties over the top of my glasses, amusing myself by trying to decide if they were on honeymoon or just in a new relationship together. They couldn't take their eyes or hands off one another, and whenever he thought no one was looking, the guy would hold or stroke her through or under her clothes; they were laughing tipsily together and looked totally blissful. It was a while before I realized that I was in turn being watched. Perched on a bar stool next to the happy couple was a guy on his own. As soon as he caught my eye I realized that he was looking at me openly and smiling, almost smirking, obviously aware that I had been spying on people. I smiled back sheepishly and looked away, but I still felt his eyes on me and when I looked back for just a split second to check, he was still watching me.

I knew what this meant. When a few minutes later a waiter approached me at the poolside with a replacement cocktail and the words, 'From the man seated at the bar', I was flattered, if not entirely surprised. Not because of arrogance, but because I was starting to learn that it is not hard to tell when a man is interested in you. If you suspect he is, he probably is. So I accepted the cocktail, smiled at Luis, and waited for things to begin.

He took his time. I was ready for another cocktail by the time he made his way over to my lounger. I had thought of going up to speak to him, but I wanted to play the game. He pulled up the chair next to me and made himself at home.

'Business or pleasure?' he asked in a lazy Spanish accent.

'Both!' I replied. He asked me how long I was staying, where I was working, and I asked the same kind of thing, a different conversation going on all the while under the surface. I watched the way he sat, leaning forward in his chair with his body towards me, and he watched my breasts and my face. It made me smile. He was just a man, a very good-looking man, and I liked the traditional kind of chase we had entered into so easily. When the waiter came back, Luis ordered us a jug of something delicious to share, and we fell into the kind of talk that can spring up between two people who are thinking mainly of sex: flirtatious discussion of ex-boyfriends and girlfriends, of people we could see on the rooftop; seamlessly on to fantasies with the next jug of cocktails.

'Why do you think you liked the couple in the bar so much?' he was asking. I had begun to tell him about my job and how it took me around the world, but had been cajoled into saying more about Paris and my revelations about sex. My fault for hinting, enticing him to ask more.

'I don't really know,' I answered truthfully. 'But it was to do with the man's expression. He knew I was watching him. He wanted me to see him touching her, and she wanted me to see it too.'

'They used you,' he teased.

'Yes! They did.' I giggled. 'I liked being used. They looked so dirty, so in the moment and it made me so horny to witness their pleasure. So private, but they made it half-public, just for me. She had her eyes closed, so she couldn't see any of me. But I could see all of her, from her exact expression to every detail of her cunt.'

He shuddered when I said the word. 'Why do you call it that?' he asked.

'I like it. It's a good, Anglo-Saxon word. It says what I want it to mean,' I told him, tipsy now, but meaning it too. 'It gets me sexy.'

'You're already sexy,' he said, and though it was naff I liked him saying it. His smile was slipping around the edges: I could tell that he was trying hard to carry on this conversation, hoping to steer it round ever closer to the goal of sex; his hard on was obvious through his trousers. I let him carry on talking.

'What did you think about when you were watching them?' he continued.

I thought carefully.

'Really nothing,' I said. 'At first I was just watching them, trying to take it in. Then I saw what was happening and I instinctively felt horny. I didn't really think anything to begin with. Then I guess I was imagining.'

'That it was you?'

'Yes. She looked how I wanted to feel.' I told him about making my way into the bathroom to touch myself, and while I was talking he leaned in and

41

simply starting kissing me. I stopped talking and kissed him back. Once our tongues touched, that was it. While we had been talking, my body had tingled with anticipation; now that we were kissing and his hands were beginning to cover me and stroke my neck, my arms, the small of my back, I felt completely alive, sensation flooding my mind. He moved a hand under my beach wrap and caressed my bare shoulder. I had been so engrossed in our conversation and our silent body language that I had not realized it had grown cool, and his hand was hot on my skin there. He picked up on it.

'Are you warm enough?'

'No,' I replied.

'Come on.' His eyes were shining. 'Let's take a dip. It will warm you up.'

I was slow to catch on and, besides, I was enjoying myself. 'No, it's fine, let's stay put.' I tried to kiss him again, but he was distracted, pulling his polo shirt over his head and unbuckling his trousers. I was momentarily alarmed, and looked round to see what the other guests thought of this, but the people that were left looked mostly engrossed in each other, or the view.

'Trust me!' he said. 'The water's lovely.' He stood almost naked now in the dusk, a gorgeous sight in tight black trunks, powerful thighs straining at the Lycra. He reached a hand out to me and grinned, so

I shrugged off my wrap and let him lead me to the water's edge.

The pool was luminous, bathed in an eerie turquoise light. The little lights from the bar spun off the water's surface, highlighting ripples. I shivered a little, and Luis beckoned me closer still. I kneeled down and put a hand into the water. He was right; it was beautifully warm, bath-like and inviting. I looked up to speak to him and saw that he had moved to the other end of the pool; I watched as he dived in, almost silently, breaking the peace of the water and causing one or two people to look round from their Bellinis before their low chattering started up again. Luis swam under the water and surfaced again at my feet. He stood and pushed his hair back, and his upper arms bulged appealingly as the muscles rose, droplets of water slipping off his skin and dancing in the light. I was mesmerized for a moment, silenced by the beauty of his physique. Luis broke the spell by reaching up and grabbing me by the waist, dragging me from the edge and into the pool with him.

He half kissed me, half danced me across the pool and backed me into a corner. 'What did I tell you?' he murmured into my ear between kisses. 'Isn't it great?' But I was distracted. I could feel him hard, firm, nudging against my thigh. I wanted him very much. Maybe I could end the game now: enough foreplay. We could go back to my room: I would just ask him outright. I was still musing on the best way to do this when I felt his fingers pull the elastic of my bikini bottoms aside and slide into my pussy. The water in the pool was nothing like the wetness there. I gasped.

'What are you doing?'

'Do you want me to stop?'

'No!'

He grinned. 'Then be quiet, little one.'

'People will see!' Even as I hissed it, I knew it sounded silly. For one, they probably wouldn't even look. Probably. And in any case, I'd spent the previous twenty minutes working us both up over a memory of just that sort of thing. Luis knew I would want to be seen, even just this once. The water rippled and splashed very gently as I wrapped my legs around his taut waist in a darkish corner of the pool and, pulling my bikini bottoms again to one side, reached for him and eased his whole length up inside me. The rush of feeling was amazing, and the water supported us both so that, leaning back into the corner, I could move myself very gently up and down on his cock. He closed his eyes, his lashes dark and wet and outlined against his cheekbone. I took in the sight of him, not letting up with my little movements, until I heard a chair scrape and, looking up, met the gaze of another man at the bar. I said nothing, but my heart beat faster, and I squeezed tighter on Luis inside me, feeling my orgasm coming close.

Luis opened his eyes and turned his head to follow my gaze. A filthy, delicious grin spread across his face. Instead of stopping, or moving us, he merely reached forward, pulling me closer around him, and began to dictate the pace, pushing me more firmly into the corner with every thrust, and reaching inside my bikini top to pinch my nipple hard. The sudden sharpness almost tipped me over the edge, and I couldn't wait any longer. I pushed my finger inside my bikini and began to circle and rub my clit hard as Luis fucked me, his mouth finding mine now. I began to shake, and felt Luis moving harder deep inside me, his tongue in my mouth and his hands grasping my arse, and Luis closed his eyes but mine were open, and locked on the gaze of the man watching us from the bar, his mouth open and his lovely face clouded with lust as I came and came, silent save for the gentle splashing of the water.

Later, much later, and still quite tipsy, I showered in my room. I felt different to the way I had in Berlin: now I felt invigorated and alive. Luis had suggested coming back with me and ordering some room-service treats, but for some reason I had gently turned him down. I think because it had been so exciting with him in the pool I didn't want to spoil that with the relative mundanity of a hotel room. Besides, I wanted adventure, to try new things; I did not want my adventures to be confined to a series of encounters in similar hotel rooms in different cities. I sang at the top of my voice in the shower, happy and full of myself, and let the hot water run over me for a long time,luxuriating in my thoughts and the feel of my tingling body.

CHAPTER 4

TOKYO

After feeling so at ease in Barcelona, Tokyo came as a shock. I was so excited about visiting Japan for the first time, especially in the famed cherry blossom season, that I had talked of nothing else for weeks beforehand. My friends and colleagues were thoroughly bored of the trip long before I actually left for it.

Japan meant fashion to me: I could only picture the capital in terms of women and clothes. I couldn't imagine how it would feel to be there in the thick of it. As soon as I arrived I realized this would be the least of my initial concerns. As I got off the plane, Japanese people ran past me at shoulder height, fast and focused. I joined the passport queue for 'Foreigners', intimidated already, and after negotiating customs spent over an hour trying to find my way into the labyrinthine underground system. The metro map I had gave English names for the stations, which was reassuring until I realized that the actual stations had no such markings. I tried to match the Japanese alphabet characters at the station with those on the maps around me, but quickly realized this was futile and escalatored myself up to ground level to hail a cab.

There was a protracted conversation about my destination, and the driver referred pointedly to his street map more than once with audible sighs, but finally I was on my way to the hotel, disorientated and tired after the twelve-hour flight.

I made my way to my room, sinking immediately into a deep sleep on a pile of slim mattresses. It wasn't until I awoke to the cheeping of my phone alarm some ten hours later that I fully took in the dainty surroundings. I never booked my own hotels – MV had an agent who sorted out all of our travel, or sometimes Paulo's assistant would choose somewhere for me – and they had impeccable taste. I had no recollection of the outside of the hotel, but this room was unmistakably Japanese, and I felt like an Oriental princess when I realized I was perched on top of eight tiny, jewel-coloured silk mattresses. The walls looked like sliding paper sheets, and the dark wood furniture was miniature. A little tea set full of steaming, fragrant jasmine tea was laid out by the side of my bed, placed there by a tiny elf as I slept, for all I knew.

Within the hour I was back in the modern world, rising up into the Tokyo branch of MV from one of the steepest escalators I had ever used. I hadn't even attempted the underground system this time, instead getting the hotel staff to book me a cab. They had grown very excited when I explained that I had to go to work at the MV store, two of the girls pointing at their shoes and hair to indicate their purchases from there. I couldn't help but wonder how front-of-house hotel staff might afford MV prices, even for accessories, but thought that perhaps they prioritized like some girls I knew at home, literally surviving on toast and tea for a month after splashing out on a handbag or coat they had fallen in love with in a magazine. Before I had worked for MV I had planned to do much the same, but a generous clothing allowance and discount meant I didn't have to make such painful sacrifices in the name of fashion.

As I came up into the heart of the store I felt the absolute foreignness of Japan hit me again. The shop floor was a sea of tiny, delicate women, each with black hair so straight and shiny they looked like beautiful dolls. The sea was broken by the occasional Western woman standing out a foot or so higher than these women, and two to four dress sizes larger. A happy, curvy size 12–14 myself, depending on my level of discipline regarding cake and lasagne from month to month, I felt enormous and clumsy here. The chatter was so alien, too: so fast, scattered with giggles and subtle bows and endless smiles. I wondered if this was how a lot of men felt back at home, trying to buy lingerie for a girlfriend for the first time, stumbling into a mysterious land of femaleness. I resolved to be more helpful if I ever saw any of these poor men in London in the future!

On my first day I suffered the most intense case of new-girl-itis you can imagine. Trying to ingratiate myself instantly in a new overseas city was not easy, but I had been pleased with how I'd got on so far, making a real effort to talk to staff and customers in each branch I'd visited, socializing with them at times and learning far more than if I'd been more reserved. Here in Tokyo, that didn't feel so much of an option. Conversation was generally slow and difficult, both parties repeating and rephrasing. While I enjoyed looking at the illustrations and plans the team showed me for the coming season, and for the planned refurbishment the following year, when it came to more detailed descriptions I had to smile politely and admit that I couldn't really understand.

The next morning started off not much better. I had woken early, and found a doughnut bar for breakfast – full of Japanese businessmen or salary-men, and smart young women, weirdly – having failed to understand the tempura breakfast menu in the restaurant window next door. The doughnuts and coffee were absolutely delicious, in fairness! Back at the shop, I sat in on a planning meeting between men I thought were other merchandisers – it was hard to tell, but two of them had brightly dyed spiky hair and colourful frames on their glasses, so I decided these were most likely part of the creative team at the branch – and the senior management.

It was an interesting experience, but I felt frustrated that I understood so little, and worried that I was letting Paulo down in terms of bringing back expertise.

But after the meeting, a slim, impeccably dressed girl I hadn't seen before approached me.

'I've been sent to rescue you,' she said. 'You've been a little bit thrown in at the deep end, I think?'

'Yes!' I practically yelled at her, gratefully. 'I'm fine, I'm fine, but I can't understand much here and also on the underground I couldn't read the signs and even in the hotel –'

She gently cut off my gabbling, placing her small hand on my forearm to calm me. 'It's OK, I have been to London. I understand. It's very hard' – she offered me a sparkling smile – 'and you want to appear professional still, I know.' She led me to another room, made me tea and the tension I hadn't even realized had built up in me over the last twenty-four hours began to seep away.

She told me her name was Teeya, and we chatted for over an hour about my limited experiences in Tokyo so far. She was sorry that she had been away for the first part of my stay, but explained that she had been visiting family in the northern part of the country. 'Now I return, and my bosses explain that it's been hard for you without a proper English speaker here to look after you.'

The words 'look after you' had a real impact on me, and the relief was so great I felt close to tears. There was something truly soothing about being in Teeya's company. When she offered to baby-sit me for the remaining two days of my trip, explaining that her seniors had given her their blessing to take me under her wing, I did not hesitate to accept.

After work that night, Teeya put me into a cab and arranged to collect me from my hotel a couple of hours later. She told me she would show me some Tokyo nightlife, and that then I would begin to understand and fall in love with the city – and she was not wrong. Teeya outside of the workplace was a very different woman. Modest and gentle at the shop, from the moment she collected me in her taxi from the hotel she was a ball of energy and fun, and full of surprises, taking me from bar to bar in the Shibuya district, each one packed more and more tightly with young Japanese people in amazing outfits. Girls wore tiny frilled and flounced skirts, socks with ribbons, eyeliner and huge hairdos; the men looked young and boyish and wore tighter clothes than the girls. It was another world. Teeya looked fabulous herself, with full make-up and a short, short black dress covered in ruffles, with red knee boots. I had dressed up too, not wanting to look dowdy as we hit the bars, but my simple shift dress and kitten heels did not compete with the full-on gothic glamour of most of the young people in the little corner of Tokyo Teeya had brought me to.

High on lychee martinis and warm saké late in the night, Teeya asked if I wanted to visit the hotels. 'But I'm already booked into one,' I said, perplexed.

'No, silly,' explained Teeya. 'There is a district especially for hotels. Love hotels. You have to see them, it's a very important side to Tokyo.'

'Love hotels?'

'Yes, for loving,' she giggled. 'The salarymen use them, and couples who haven't got their own place . . . there's nothing to be ashamed of. They're all tucked away on discreet streets. You pay by the night or also the hour, for a rest.' We both laughed. 'A rest?' I asked, not believing her entirely.

'You know. No? Come on, I'll show you.'

With an ease I could only wonder at, Teeya flagged down a taxi, and within seconds we were whizzing to another part of town. Teeya dragged me by the hand from the cab, and practically ran with me around a corner and up a little hill, and sure enough, there was a tiny village of fantastical buildings: Egyptian palaces, Vegas-style hide-outs, sumptuous European castles; each in miniature and lit up like fireworks. Each promised Rests and Stays, some offering Love Costumes and Toys for hire, some less coy and offering Dildos and Viblaters (I kid you not) and even Hardcore Porn, brazen as you like. Teeya laughed at my open mouth as we explored the narrow streets further and I tried to take in the sea of photographs showing what appeared to be waterfalls in some of the hotels' rooms, and thrones and dungeon setups in some of the others.

Teeya pulled me close suddenly in a doorway in one of the streets. 'My treat,' she whispered in my ear. 'You should experience one of these rooms while you're here!'

I was taken aback. For a moment I thought she was propositioning me, and then I realized that she was just being tipsy and flirtatious. 'Fuck it,' I thought, and forgot myself, throwing myself back into the adventurous spirit of the night, and I let her book us into one of the hotels, tapping into a machine in the wall until a discreet little man led us to a room along a corridor decorated randomly with fake Hawaiian flowers and paintings of lions and tropical forests.

I laughed out loud when we entered the room. A vast bed occupied most of the space, and a range of buttons and levers on a control panel above the head-board made the room look retro and space age. A large plasma TV on the wall clicked on as we locked the door, and porn-style music started up automatically alongside some credits on the screen.

'I can't believe this place,' I laughed delightedly, turning to face Teeya. But she had stopped laughing. Her expression unsettled me, but I also began to feel a pounding in my heart and stomach that was not entirely unwelcome. Saying nothing, she walked closer to me and reached for me, kissing me on the mouth and thrusting her hand into my hair.

I had never even thought about kissing a girl before. Well. Not strictly true. But I had never really imagined it happening, and it felt amazing. Teeya's tongue was both gentle and enthusiastic, searching my mouth and making my skin tingle. Her lips were soft and her breath minty and delicious, a million miles from crushing male mouths and the smell of beer or whisky I associated with 'proper snogging'.

After endless minutes Teeya pulled away and looked into my face. She was obviously pleased with what she saw there: my expression must have shown my pleasure and, encouraged, she pulled me gently on to the bed. Distant moans came from the screen before us, but I suddenly only had eyes for Teeya. There was so much to think about, but I tried to switch off all thought and enjoy the moment. I wondered if we would only kiss, and felt a surprising stab of disappointment; I wanted to see all of her, to touch her fragile beauty and possess her. I need not have feared. Teeya began to take off her dress in front of me and I watched in awe: her body was breathtaking. With her dark straight hair and blunt fringe highlighting her lovely features, she was beautiful anyway, but as she revealed the clean lines of her body I took in her silky golden skin, her pert breasts, her flat stomach and narrow waist and hips. Everything was so different to my own figure, but before I could compare, Teeya was behind me, unzipping my shift dress and reaching round to cup my breasts through my bra. She seemed amazed at their size, saying nothing but gasping and smiling and almost weighing them, and pulling the bra aside at the front to pinch a nipple hard. It responded immediately, thrusting at her fingers eagerly, and she moved round in front of me again and bent over to take it in her mouth. In the mirror I could see the reflection of her bottom, small and tight like the rest of her, and made more adorable by the little V of her black panties above the slimness of her thighs in their hold-up stockings.

Everything moved so slowly and silkily it was almost like a dream. I could feel myself wet, so wet between my thighs as Teeya kissed and gently bit my nipple. I put out a tentative hand to stroke her bare shoulder and back, and, even in the warm room, shivered with pleasure at the feel of her skin. She looked up from one breast, the other filling her palm, and smiled at me again, and I drew her towards me, kissing her hard on the mouth and running an experimental hand over that firm arse, slipping a finger into the band of her knickers and then between her legs.

I had no idea what I would feel at that moment, but she was nothing like me. Where I knew my own pussy was pretty but fluffy, with curly dark hair, Teeya had barely any down on her; she felt naked and wet between her legs, welcoming and exciting. She parted her legs slightly and I slid a finger deep inside her, groaning in a wave of sudden pleasure and desire. I clung on to her body, kissing her mouth and tongue and bending briefly to bite one of her own small nipples. She pulled me back and spread her thighs wide, murmuring my name and pushing me down her body. I felt a moment's nerves and then buried my face between her legs, tasting her carefully at first and lapping like a cat at her neat little cunt, and then shoving my tongue inside, pushing it inside her as hard and as far as I could before pulling out and lapping at her again, flicking my tongue over her clit the way I remembered more experienced men doing to me. She began to moan louder and more rhythmically, and I carried on but ran a hand up her inner thigh, and stroked her just for a moment before sliding two fingers into her while I licked. Teeya bucked and grew louder, and I decided not to care about the neighbouring room as I flicked my tongue harder and Teeya began to come noisily under my mouth.

I watched Teeya quietly as she lay back on the bed afterwards, trying to catch her breath. I did not know what might happen next, but thankfully she recovered herself and threw me a naughty smile. 'You lay back now,' she commanded, and I did as I was told while I heard her rummaging in a drawer. She pulled out a long box and held it in the air dramatically. 'Do you like these?' she asked.

I had no idea what it was and, seeing my expression, she unwrapped the box and pulled out a large, rubbery-looking purple dildo. It looked a bit like a normal vibrator, but much too big, and seemed to have two ends to it. My imagination began to run.

'These are great,' she announced enthusiastically. She approached me almost coldly, pushing my legs apart and staring between my thighs as though sizing me up. 'You can take it, I think,' she said, half to herself, and I gasped as without warning she eased the wide dildo far up inside me. My pussy contracted around it: I was horny, and I wanted to come, but it was not enough. 'Oh, sweetie,' she said, faking concern but looking very mischievous indeed. 'Come on, I'll share with you.'

Teeya came closer, straddling my thighs. She took the end of the dildo and pushed it to and fro inside me for a few strokes, making me groan out in pleasure and frustration. It was too big, bigger than any man I had ever had, and I felt absolutely stretched. I needed my clit to be touched, partly to distract me from the feeling inside my pussy but mainly because I was desperate to come. Seeing my desperation, Teeya stopped fucking me with the dildo, but moved closer still. I saw a look of concentration cross her face, and then watched amazed as she put the free tip of the dildo between her own legs, rubbed her clit with it for a few seconds, and then her expression changed as she slipped the whole remaining length inside her own cunt.

I could not quite work out what had happened at first. My pussy now touched Teeya's, rubbed right up against its own slipperiness, and we were so close – closer than I think I had ever felt to anyone, impaled on the same length. I felt a tiny shudder as she squeezed her muscles around the dildo, squatting over me. Her face was pink with excitement, her breath coming fast. I could barely breathe. It felt so dirty, so hot and contrived and amazing, and then she began to rise and fall, pulling the thing to and fro between us, crashing down on my clit rhythmically for what felt like forever but can only in reality have been minutes before I began to feel overwhelmed. I reached up and clutched Teeya in my arms and closed my eyes as my whole cunt began to throb with uncontrollable pleasure, the stretch inside me now matched by waves of sensation . . . I think I must have blacked out, for when I came to Teeya was grinning at the end of the bed, fully dressed.

'How did you enjoy your Rest?' she asked naughtily. She was affectionate with me, chatting to me while I showered and rubbing my aching thigh muscles before helping me to drag my clothes back on, then we checked out of the tiny love hotel and stepped into the night. Teeya found me my last taxi of the night and kissed me goodbye.

CHAPTER 5

NEW YORK

I thought about Teeya a lot after that night. At work the next day I had found it hard to concentrate: what had happened changed the way I thought about myself. I had assumed I was entirely straight, for a start, and now I didn't really even know what that meant. Did one night change that? Did it change it a little bit? Would it just become something to tease future boyfriends with? I decided that I wouldn't let it, but I also knew myself well enough to know I'd find it hard to resist getting guys excited with details of our night together. For a while I harboured fantasies about seeing Teeya again, even being her girlfriend. We could go shopping together, buy each other make-up treats, maybe share a little flat in London, Tokyo or New York . . .

But I got back into my work, and back into the rhythm of my London life, and thoughts of Teeya began to fade away. She emailed me fairly often, and I liked swapping news and thoughts with her and hoped we could stay close. Maybe even have occasional adventures together. But overall I wanted to move forward, with my career and my experiments, and I didn't want to stop to think about complicated things like feelings and attachments too much.

In retrospect, meeting Daniel on my New York trip was almost inevitable. I was growing more and more adventurous, determined to push myself farther beyond my previous sexual boundaries, buoyed up and also shaken by what had passed between Teeya and me: I had liked her a little too much for comfort. It had been so rude and intimate and exciting, being with her. I think I also needed to reassure myself that I still fancied men, enjoyed sleeping with them and liked the gaps in male-to-female communication that made for mystery and confusion.

I had been absolutely thrilled when Paulo asked me to go to the Big Apple for the shows, and couldn't wait to throw myself into the social life there. I knew from other employees that the staff at the NYC branch were all pretty outgoing; that the men were mostly gay, *loved* dancing and fashion; and that the store had excellent links and contacts with people at the city's most influential magazines. I needed to focus back on work – and this would be such a brilliant opportunity for me. But I didn't bet on meeting Daniel.

I was enjoying an unseasonal and huge frothy hot chocolate at Heathrow airport when I first saw him. His suit caught my eye; I know enough about cut to know that this was a very expensive suit indeed, with its beautifully subtle tailoring and peeping pink silk lining. As my eye travelled up and I took in dark tousled hair, flecked with grey, skimming gorgeous cheekbones and silver-rimmed glasses, I felt myself skip a breath. He was talking to a shop assistant and she was blooming and squirming under his easy smile. I felt a stab of illogical jealousy, which I should have read as a warning sign, but chose to ignore.

An hour later, laden with impulse airport purchases of sparkly eye shadow and a slightly-cheaper-than-usual-but-still-out-of-my-price-range new handbag, I clambered on to the plane. It was a cool, extremely blowy day, and I really battled up the rickety stairs on to the flight, clutching carrier bags in one hand, hat to head with the other, hand luggage stuffed under my arm. I stumbled down the central aisle, looking for row D and wishing MV were generous enough (or that I was important enough to MV already) to pay for business-class seats for my trips. For a moment I thought I saw him there, sitting inevitably in my row, and I panicked because I knew I must look windblown and harassed, rather than the sexy international jetsetter I wanted to seem. But then a second glance revealed him to be just an ordinary guy: not at all the man who had so turned my head earlier.

After this unpromising start the flight passed quickly, without incident or – sadly – upgrade. At JFK

I looked around nonchalantly for my man in the suit, having brushed my hair and even swapped my specs for contact lenses in the ladies, despite my eyes feeling raw with tiredness. But there was no sign of him. There was no guarantee he was even heading for New York, I knew, even though he looked as though he should be, and had been walking through the airport in the right direction. But somehow I didn't feel disappointed. I felt as though this was a temporary hitch, because I would surely be seeing him again, somewhere, somehow. And I was right.

The MV store in New York was amazing. Just as I had been impressed by the sleek, understated glamour of the branch in Tokyo, here I was blown away by the full-on colour and exuberance of the shop. There was no mistaking it as the same company, same label, but here there was a completely different atmosphere. The shop suited its location in the newly glam meat-packing district, nestled among neglected-looking buildings and swish warehouse conversions; industrial structures and gorgeous boutique shops. Despite the hot weather the sky was grey and overcast, swollen with clouds, and this only added to the run-down, edgy beauty of the place.

I worked a long shift that first day at the branch. I had to be at MV for nine in the morning, despite having arrived late at night, and was determined to appear fresh and focused. It wasn't as hard as I might have thought. The sheer energy of the place carried me along. In London, there was often a sombre kind of atmosphere in the Bond Street shop. People often took the business of spending money seriously, and demanded the same of the staff. This was different: the men and women who came in treated it as fun, and the people who worked there showed the same sense of proportion and enthusiasm for the luxuries they sold.

Maurice (pronounced Mor-reece!), who ran the store, thought it would be good for me to get to know the New York clientele, and he was right: it was a complete education. Yes, the customers enjoyed their shopping, but they demanded a lot of attention – this applied mainly to the New Yorkers themselves, but by osmosis also the other American and European shoppers who thronged through the store. The policy at the branch was to indulge, spoil and adore customers, whether that meant laughing at their jokes for over an hour or making tea for them while they tried on shoes. By the time the shop shut and we'd had an end-of-day briefing, part of me was desperate to get back to my hotel room and sleep. But as soon as we tied up the last agenda point, Simon and Peter – two of the guys in buying – let out a whoop and announced that it was time to throw on some disco tunes and get OUT!

'Where shall we take you, Eleanor?'

'What do you want to see?'

'What have you got to wear?'

Their questions crowded in on me, and I confessed I'd only had the wit that morning to bring in some mascara and a change of shoes, in case there were any after-work drinks.

'Poor Eleanor! Is this how we do things in London?' laughed Simon, the older of the two men. 'My gosh, get the girl some glad rags. In back,' he gestured to Peter. 'Thank God we have supplies,' he announced melodramatically, and I laughed as Peter came running back minutes later with a red velvet MV cushion bearing a range of beautifully packaged make-up, and some clothes draped over his arm.

'Sweetie, you *shall* go to the ball,' Simon told me.

I picked through the array of expensive-looking tops and dresses at my disposal.

'Where did all this stuff come from?' I asked.

'Oh, various,' Peter said airily. 'Some, gifts from customers. Others just stuff people left behind. You know, if they want to wear the new garment right away.'

'Then they would just leave it here?' I asked disbelievingly.

'For sure! You know, out of excitement for the new thing. They just step out of what they're wearing;

leave it on the shop floor, in some instances. You wonder how they end their relationships . . . We launder it all, honey, I promise!'

I laughed again, amazed that people would give away or abandon these luxury items. I had seen nothing like this in London – local customers there would make sure they returned even to collect the most dog-eared of umbrellas! By the time I had pulled on a clingy grey jersey dress, tried out some of the cosmetics and 'borrowed' some super-soft MV hold-ups, Peter and Simon deemed me perfectly worthy of a night out at one of their favourite clubs, Secrecy.

'Secrecy? It sounds like a lap-dancing club,' I half joked. 'Are you sure?'

'Trust us,' Peter said. 'It's been going for a long time. It's elegant, Eleanor, not a lap in sight. Well' – they both sniggered – 'not a lap dance, anyway. You're not attached or anything unpleasant, are you?'

I thought briefly of Teeya, and unexpectedly of Johnny, my ex. 'No,' I confirmed, 'I'm free. I'm up for anything!'

'I'd keep that to yourself, dear, at least at first,' Simon told me. 'Come on, everyone, it's time!' He clapped his hands, and other staff who'd been in corners applying make-up and styling their hair, some even pressing their shirts, came out of the shadows to reveal themselves as glorious peacocks, and we set off into the night.

And that was where I saw him again. I had been in Secrecy – every bit as lovely as promised – for all of five minutes when I saw his face, and my heart flipped in my chest. I was shocked by the physical impact this utter stranger had on me – and by how much I did not want us to remain strangers.

I didn't dare approach him at first. After securing a round of gin cocktails for us all – 'No calories in gin, darling, drink up' – Simon herded the little group of us towards the dance floor. Without any warm-up, most people threw themselves energetically into the throng, and began shimmying and moving in a way I loved to see. I adored dancing myself, and was soon lost in retro disco beats, warmed by gin and the euphoric atmosphere.

Within half an hour, I was hot and sweaty and happy, and had found my man again. I saw him across the dance floor, not dancing but observing, and I made my way closer to him without letting him see I was watching him. I thought.

He turned his back briefly to order from the bar, and again I found myself watching too avidly the way he spoke to the barmaid, talking low so she had to come in close, making her giggle while he maintained his cool. When he turned around, I quickly moved my eyes away, wanting him to watch me, not daring to look to see if he was. When I eventually did look back, he was gone – and then, as fast as my heart had begun to sink, it leaped again when I heard a voice at my ear.

'What's a girl like you doing in a big gay bar like this?' he asked in a charming New York accent.

I spun round and couldn't help but grin with pleasure just to see him close up. 'It's not just gay, is it?' I asked. 'And what are you doing here if it is?'

'Looking for you,' he said simply, and without thinking or caring too much about the consequences I kissed him full on the mouth. 'Good,' I said. Forgetting my new colleagues, forgetting everything, I suddenly wanted nothing more than to take this man back to my hotel and feel his body against, inside, mine. He kissed me back, and then pulled away.

'That's a little forward, don't you think?' he asked, and I felt my cheeks blush.

'Sorry,' I mumbled, suddenly confused. 'I –'

'Shhh. I like you. I don't want to embarrass you. Are you still here tomorrow?'

'Here?'

'Manhattan. How long are you here with your shop work?'

'Huh? How do you know –'

'Stop asking questions, kiddo! Are you here tomorrow night?'

I nodded.

'Then I'll take you out. I'll come and get you from your hotel at nine. OK? Is nine OK?'

'Yes . . .'

'Marvellous. I have to shoot. I'll see you then.' And he was gone, leaving me ecstatic but wondering how the hell he knew where my hotel was, and just how much more he knew about me.

The next day, the guys and some of the women at work were intrigued. 'Be careful,' a girl called Lottie warned me. 'He must be married. Or maybe he's a stalker.'

'Or both?' chimed in Simon.

But I felt no panic, just a thrill of excitement that extended all the way from my scalp to my toes at the thought of seeing him again, and made another long, hard day feel like it lasted no more than an hour.

By nine o'clock that night I was buffed, bathed, fragrant and looking as good as I could for him. The phone in my room rang, dead on the hour.

'It's Daniel,' he said.

'Daniel,' I repeated, dumbly. I said it again silently to myself. Daniel. 'Hello, Daniel,' I said. 'It's Eleanor. Shall I come down?'

With that though, there was a noise at the door – the sound of a lock opening – and Daniel walked straight into my room, mobile in hand. 'No, I'll come and get you,' he said to my face. My mouth fell open, and then into a grin at his sheer cheek and cunning. I decided not to question him.

'I brought you something to wear,' he announced. I was amazed – what a man! He came nearer, and asked me to shut my eyes. He kissed me gently, and I heard a little click. He brushed my hair away from my neck and I felt something encircle my throat, and smiled with pleasure at such an old-fashioned, romantic beginning to a date. 'Look in the mirror,' Daniel murmured, but when I did, what I saw filled me with confusion and unease.

I looked to Daniel for an explanation but he only smiled, a beautiful, powerfully reassuring smile. 'It's OK,' he insisted. 'Take another peep. Don't panic; try to keep an open mind.'

I turned again to the mirror and tried to make sense of what I could see. There I was, glamorous enough in my most flattering black dress, cut away at the front to reveal most of my generous, round breasts; and there next to me was Daniel, dark and serene in another impeccable suit. And there, around my neck, was a thick silver collar, and there around Daniel's wrist – showing clearly as he held up his white shirt cuff – was a finer band of silver, and there between the two was a thick metallic rope, joining us, binding us to within three feet of one another.

'This is locked,' he said. 'You can tell me now if you'd like me to unlock you, and I promise to do just that, and leave you in peace, and send you some flowers and an apology for scaring you.'

I paused, not sure if my voice would hold out. 'And if I don't?'

'If you don't?'

'If I don't tell you to unlock me. If I trust you. What happens then?'

My heart was pounding, but I wasn't scared. The fact is, I felt alive. Fear had already faded, and been replaced by excitement. I *did* trust Daniel; that was the thing. I had no real reason to, but I felt safe with him, and I knew that whatever he wanted from me that evening I might just want to go along with. My mind was filling with such filthy thoughts and fantasies, all stemming from the simple act of him placing a collar round my neck, that all decisions seemed simple. Show me, my silent inner voice screamed. Show me everything you know. I want to learn.

Daniel looked at me intently. 'If you are sure,' he said, 'then we could play. I promise not to hurt you. Even if you ask me to. We'll play, and in a few hours' time I can bring you back here, and you'll just have had an interesting evening. But there are some rules.'

'What are the rules?' I breathed, much too eager even at this stage.

'You have to let go. No games. No trying to get my attention on the dance floor' – he put his hand to my mouth to silence my defence and smiled – 'you have to behave. For one night, you won't be able to enjoy the freedom your gay friends or the other young women do. You will see something different of the city, and of yourself, and you won't speak unless I say you can. Can you agree to that?'

I thought for a moment. Was this safe? How could I look after myself if I did not speak? But of course I *would* be able to speak. I only had to obey his rules for as long as I wanted to play the game. If I wanted to, I could scream, or cry out, or speed-dial on my mobile. And I trusted him. And I was intrigued. So I nodded.

His face lit up.

'Then we'll start,' he said, and kissed me. 'Come on.'

He led me out of the hotel room and down the corridor. We passed two hotel employees and another couple on our way out, all of whom stared and looked mildly disgusted at the sight of the collar on my bare neck and the chain, but who said nothing. I blushed again, and felt a tingling between my legs.

In the lift, Daniel kissed me again. An older, single male got in at one of the floors on the way down and, instead of stopping what he was doing, Daniel slipped a hand down the front of my dress and pinched my nipple. I yelped despite myself, and he did it again, but this time I stifled the noise, and Daniel let go of me. I saw the man watching us in the mirror, his face a picture, but the three of us remained in silence all the way to the ground floor, when the man looked at me again as he got out, his features still shocked but full of interest and lust.

We had not even left the hotel and I felt hot with desire. The tiny incident in the lift – not even two minutes had passed on the way down – had made me crazy with need. Daniel led me outside the hotel and put his hand out, clearly revealing the chain between us. 'Taxi,' he called out, and a yellow cab pulled up immediately. He ushered me in and we sat in silence for a moment. 'Well?' asked the driver. 'Where to?' His words were as brusque as any cab driver's, but in the rear-view mirror his face looked unusually pleased.

'Just up the road,' said Daniel. 'Or around, for a while.'

Naturally I thought this odd, but I was determined to stick to the rules. I said nothing. Daniel squeezed my hand affectionately. 'Open your legs a little,' he said.

I bit back a shocked response. He had made no attempt to lower his voice. My eyes flicked again to the rear-view mirror, but the driver was not looking. I did as I was told.

'Good girl,' said Daniel. 'Little bit more.'

I took a shallow breath and moved my thighs wider apart. This time the driver looked into the mirror and smiled. It was an easy, pleasant smile. He was not shocked. Puzzled, I kept my feelings to myself, and wondered how much the driver could already see.

'Lift your bottom,' Daniel ordered, and as I did so he reached beneath me, tugged at my panties and began to ease them down over my thighs. He made slow progress, and I heard his breathing, easy and controlled. I also heard the other breathing, the driver's, and as I looked up I saw he was flicking his eyes from the road and back to me. I raised my legs to let Daniel slip the silky knickers off over my patent heels.

'I think I'd better let you out,' the cabbie said shortly.

Moments later we were stepping from the cab into the road, my underwear in Daniel's pocket. I noticed that Daniel didn't pay for the ride, and had to remind myself not to question it. I wasn't sure where we were, and was surprised when Daniel stopped a few steps down and rang on a buzzer. The building looked like offices to me, so I was even more surprised when an old man in a bow tie answered the door.

'Ah, beautiful,' said the old man, looking me up and down. 'What's her name?'

He welcomed us in, taking us both by the hand and leading us up some stairs as he did so.

'Eleanor,' said Daniel. 'She's new to all this.'

'But of course,' said the man. 'I'm Albert, by the way. How rude of me.' I smiled at him. I felt as though I were in a dream, as the two men led me up a grand staircase. Both were so gentle and well mannered.

I wondered whether I should feel afraid, but instead I felt an unreal serenity, as though putting on the collar had been a symbolic act, and I was no longer responsible for my actions. Not speaking, too, meant that I was living through my impressions of the evening much more intensely. I took in the contrast between the industrial exterior of the building and the sumptuous, domestic interior as we mounted the stairs and came out into a large, empty, warm hall. It looked and felt much like a traditional London gentlemen's club: the thick carpet; the rich, dark decoration; the portraits of old, white men on the walls.

Daniel indicated for me to stop for a moment. 'We'll go through now,' he said gently. 'There's nothing to be afraid of. You'll like it a lot, I promise.' I smiled at him, giving away nothing. Albert walked to two high, thick doors at the far end of the hall, and pushed them open. Immediately the air was filled with noise; beyond the doors I could see people, many people, standing together dressed as formally as Albert, men and women. Daniel led the way ahead, into the room.

At first, nothing seemed too unusual. I was shy of the chain but also aroused by the idea that everyone would assume I was totally at the mercy of Daniel's whim. He was a good-looking man and really did look sharp in his suit, and as we entered, people's gazes lingered on him before turning to me and looking me up and down approvingly – men and women alike – much as Albert had done at the door.

I was so self-conscious and obsessed with what people would think of me that at first I failed to return their gaze. Daniel led me across the full length of the room, and settled me at the back of it in an ancient-looking wooden chair.

'What do you think?' he asked, gesturing across the swarming room to me. 'Don't the women look radiant?'

I had mainly been watching the men, enjoying their elegant suits and the confident way they all seemed to hold themselves. But as I focused more on the women, I noticed that each wore a collar just like mine, and was tethered to a man. In fact, looking closer still, I saw more than one woman whose collar led to the wrists of two different men, one either side.

I turned back to Daniel to reply. 'I don't understand. Is everyone the same? Has everyone been kidnapped for the night?' I said this with a twinkle, but he looked pained at the suggestion.

'Please, I want you to enjoy yourself. Tell me now if you're not comfortable,' he whispered. 'I won't mind. But tell me now for sure – I won't ask again, or else you won't be able to relax.'

I spoke honestly. 'I want to stay. I don't want to be anywhere else but here, with you.' He smiled with relief, and kissed me briefly, stroking my hair.

'We'll say no more about it, then,' he said. 'Now be quiet, and watch over there. Some people are starting already.'

I opened my mouth to ask, 'Starting what?' but remembered myself and closed it again. I looked where Daniel had pointed. A couple were standing on a raised platform – too small to be called a stage, but a little area not five feet square, with a chair in the middle, which the couple stood to the side of. As we watched, the man took the chair, slowly, slowly, and tugged at his wrist, forcing the woman to come closer. He angled his wrist once again, and pulled her gently towards his lap. For a moment I was utterly shocked, surprised at the idea that we might see something as graphic as a blow job, but then the woman moved at her partner's coaxing into a position across his lap, and I understood.

The man sat bolt upright with the woman bent entirely across him, her blonde hair now hiding her face as it almost touched the ground, her bottom in its neat black pencil skirt directly in his lap. Her knees were bent and her toes just skimmed the floor. Her body looked surprisingly relaxed, even when he leaned back and reached into his pocket to pull out a length of white rope, and then moved her hands behind her back. I could barely breathe with excitement, and squeezed Daniel's hand.

Once the woman's palms were bound tightly together, I could see that she was utterly trapped.

Her partner smiled at the crowd, and a low murmur of appreciation ran around the room as he began to draw her skirt up to reveal slender thighs and a neat, bare bottom under a black suspender belt.

With the utmost leisure, he drew his own palm a foot or two up into the air and then brought it down again, hard, on the woman's skin. She juddered slightly, and I realized again I was holding my breath. I shifted a little in my seat, wet between my thighs already.

The man repeated the act slowly. He brought his hand up once, twice, three, four times more, on the fourth slap staying his hand a moment to cause her – and me, and all the silent audience – to wait for the satisfying thwack on her arse. She was mostly silent herself during this time, but as the man began to increase both the speed and strength of his smacks she cried out more than once. Even from where I was sitting, some thirty feet away, I could see that her skin had begun to blush pink.

Just when I thought I couldn't bear it any longer, and would have to try to excuse myself from Daniel to go to the bathroom and make myself come, the little show stopped. I was sorry: I found myself wanting to see the man slap her harder and harder, make her cry out more for my pleasure. It was almost that I wanted to see her humiliated on the stage; for him to take things further. I looked briefly at the other couples; they looked similarly entranced and full of anticipation.

I needn't have worried. As the man helped the blonde gracefully to her feet, and led her down slowly from the stage, I saw other people walk towards them. As though it were the most normal thing in the world, and with a brief word to her partner, one man reached out and began to unbutton her dress. She stood stock still and silent as the stranger removed the dress completely, and other men drew closer with their tethered women to see better. Daniel slowly got up, forcing me to rise too and follow him into the middle of the room.

She had an amazing figure. Tall and slender, her breasts were small in their pretty bra but very pert. Another man reached around behind her to undo her bra, and the nipples sprang free, hard and pink; the first man ran a palm gently across them, and the second followed him, cupping a bare breast in his hand before stroking it lovingly and watching the nipple tighten further still. She remained standing, knickerless in stockings and suspenders and neck collar, a traditional fantasy picture made all the more so by the expression of bliss on her face. She was with us but not with us: a beautiful thing to play with, silently happy just to be touched, moulded, with nothing but pleasure written on her face.

Her partner intervened briefly and turned her round to face the back of the room. He bent her gently at the waist and of course she obliged. There was a sharp intake of breath in the room; at this angle, we could all now clearly see the line of her bare vagina. It glistened beautifully, plump and wet with her excitement at being spanked and now paraded. Another man stepped forward and licked two fingers before bringing his hand between her legs and rubbing her exposed cunt slowly, ever so slowly, making the woman gasp with pleasure and push her bottom out closer towards his hand.

'Slut,' laughed her partner, and slapped her pink bottom again. The other man rubbed his fingers to and fro as the woman moaned, shifting on her high heels in obvious arousal, although of course we could not now see her face.

Then this man stepped back – I thought about how hard he must be – and gestured politely for the man next to him to have a turn. This man shook his head, but whispered in the ear of the woman tied to his wrist. The couple moved in and the woman sank to her knees before the blonde.

Fully dressed, she caressed the blonde's bottom before parting the woman's legs so that all could properly see her cunt's wet pinkness. My own legs felt shaky now. Then the kneeling woman put her face into the blonde's exposed pussy and began to lap furiously; within seconds of this sudden assault the room reverberated with mounting cries of relief and pleasure as the blonde shook and trembled and came. When she finally fell silent the room filled with whoops and claps.

For the first time since the second part of the show had begun I looked at Daniel. He still looked elegant, but his face was flushed too: his eyes were glazed with desire.

'Don't you need the bathroom?' he asked urgently, and I was about to ask him to let me go when I saw what he meant. I nodded, and he began to lead me across the room, but we bumped into a man I immediately recognized as the driver of our cab, with a young black girl of about twenty.

'What a surprise!' said the cab driver. 'How are you enjoying the show so far? This is Elise.' He encouraged her to greet me, and she kissed me on both cheeks.

Daniel spoke for me.

'She likes it a lot. We were just going through to the cloakroom, if you'd like to come? Eleanor, by the way, this is James, now you're meeting properly.'

I smiled politely and kissed James on the cheek, but adrenaline was coursing through me again. Come with us? To the cloakroom? I had no idea exactly what Daniel meant. I badly wanted to have sex – my pussy was hot and very ready from watching the show, and

I knew it would not take me long but that I must come, soon. I did not know how I felt about someone else, or another couple, watching or being a part of that, but on the other hand I felt so desperate to have my orgasm I didn't really think I would care.

Before I could think about this any longer, Daniel ushered the four of us onward and through a side door to a little room set up like a boudoir. There was a freestanding bath in the middle of the room, and two chairs beside it; the room was very warm thanks to a real fire burning low in the grate. Most of the walls were covered with ornate antique mirrors, and the four of us were reflected, multiplied by tens, back into the room.

Daniel kissed me on the mouth as James shut the door and took a seat, and began to undress me. I did not resist. 'She's lovely,' James said, as my breasts swung free from my bra. I was not wearing knickers, of course, and I was so excited that Daniel's hand shone wet just skimming my pussy as he pushed my skirt down over my thighs. 'Can I touch her?' asked James quietly. 'By all means,' Daniel muttered, but James had already moved in and slid his fingers into my aching cunt.

My disappointment at not being touched by Daniel left me in seconds, as my senses filled and popped with pleasure at the relief of the other man's touch. He eased me gently to the edge of the bath and I sat with my thighs splayed wide as James moved his fingers in a circular motion over my clit, then back into my pussy, pushing them further and firmer and back over my clit. I could not bear it. I looked at Daniel, who squeezed my hand and nodded encouragingly, and I shut my eyes tight and succumbed to the sensation, moving myself further on to James's hand as I came in waves and moaned with enjoyment.

When I opened my eyes I felt some of the reality of the situation sink in and I was shocked at myself, but the other three grinned at me, and I laughed with surprise and relief that the atmosphere was so easy after such intimacy. Daniel spoke quietly to James, and then gently moved me round, fumbling in his pocket for a condom and then bending me over the bath, and the last thing I saw as he thrust himself hard into me and began to fuck me was hundreds of reflections of the other couple, her astride him with her beautiful back to me, rising up and down on a chair in a corner of the room in rhythm with Daniel and me.

It would take me a long time to understand how much my time with Daniel had changed me. The perfect gentleman, he had driven me to the airport himself two days later, treating me to brunch and telling me to take care of myself. There was no reference to what had happened before, except for a naughty look in Daniel's eyes, and a constant tenderness between us, a closeness that had come from nowhere and settled over us like a warm blanket. What we had experienced together had passed, but perhaps it would come again; I thought of little else on the plane back to London. Things that I had thought simple were clouding even as I turned them over in my head. The delicate balance of power between men and women, for instance: it could be played with, worked to advantage; but it would be easily shattered by a clumsy word or action. Before, had I thought about it, I would have said that humiliation should play no part in sex. Now, I felt uneasily – naughtily – that this was not always the case. Everything had its place, given the right circumstances. A man or woman with charisma, a couple with the right chemistry: these could be the right circumstances for any number of pleasurable games. I was learning, then, learning all the time.

CHAPTER 6

ROME

It was autumn before it was time to go away again. I had enjoyed late August in England; it was warm and familiar, and the weekends were a time for me to be lazy and recuperate. Whenever I was overseas, I couldn't wait to see my girlfriends again; friends from my art foundation course in London, or my uni in Bristol, and of course I was having such amazing adventures on my trips that I couldn't wait to share them. But then I would meet with my friends, for lunch, or in a bar, or just chatting on and on over wine and bad films in scruffy lounges, and it would seem wrong to start talking about how much I was loving my career or my international travel. Or – in particular – my secret life fucking strange men and women in foreign cities.

Funny, that one. I just couldn't work out how to broach these subjects with any sense of normality. It was another world; so separate from my summer social life with my friends, watching tennis in parks, or staying inside when it rained, with *Pretty Woman* and an oven pizza. So in the end, I decided to keep it private. Sometimes I would tell funny or daft anecdotes – describing the time I almost missed the connecting train on the way to the airport in Berlin, and had to take off my stilettos in the station and run all the way over the bridge in my tights to catch it. Or about the time I told the floor manager of the Barcelona branch that I couldn't fax a particular document to him because I needed to keep the original.

Essentially, I told them about things or events that made me look stupid. I felt too self-conscious and boastful to tell them much about the frankly amazing sights I had seen; the bars in Tokyo and New York I had loved; the different people I had slept with, of both genders. My friends in the UK didn't really know this side of me – of course, I was only just getting used to it myself – and I didn't want to spoil the closeness we had by highlighting the differences between their student lives, or twelve-thousand-a-year starter arts jobs, and my own rather more glamorous and other-worldly experiences.

So by the time my trip to Rome rolled around, I had begun to grow used to my old life again. By not talking about exactly what I busied myself with on my trips, I began to forget and see them almost as vague memories or daydreams. Almost as though they had happened to someone else, and I had merely heard about them.

Flying to Rome brought back many of the memories – vividly so. The black cab to the airport; the thick chocolate or latte in a café there; the last-minute shopping and the reading-up of notes for whatever MV headquarters I was going to visit; all of these were little rituals I observed on every trip. I had a particularly busy schedule for Rome – there were to be lots of fashion parties that I was invited (and expected!) to attend, and the shop itself was by all accounts going into meltdown with the levels of interest and footfall their new collection was receiving. I had my work head firmly back on: if I met a hot young Italian boy while I was out there then that might be lovely, but sex was not my priority for this trip. Really!

New York had exhausted me, and while I hadn't taken time to really analyse everything that happened under Daniel's wing while I was there, I knew I had really pushed myself. I had crossed some boundaries that previously felt natural to me, and while I felt this was a good thing, it still made me blush to think of the tone of his voice, or the cab ride with James and what had happened later. Daniel was still in touch, emailing and ordering me to return to see him as soon as I could. I wanted to, but since I'd been home it had also felt good to pull back and reclaim some control. As a result, actually, I hadn't enjoyed more than a snog back in the UK, so I suppose it wasn't surprising that sex should creep back on to my agenda in Rome just as soon as I was reminded of its potency.

On my second morning in Rome I was asked by the shop manager to work in menswear. I was happy to do this; they were extremely busy and I was doing enough creative merchandising work and attending meetings in the afternoon to make spending mornings on the shop floor quite enjoyable. I didn't know much about menswear, however, and while I was pleased for the opportunity to fill in some gaps, I was a little nervous about how demanding the customers would be.

But at the risk of generalizing, the Italian men who came in to shop either knew exactly what they wanted, and merely used me to carry goods to and from them in the plush changing suites, or were more interested in chatting to me than the details of the clothes they were looking at. One gorgeous older guy simply asked me for some black trousers and three black cashmere jumpers in his size, and then kept me chatting about England for three-quarters of an hour. But then a slightly more awkward customer came in. It started off well enough; he asked for help choosing an outfit for a wedding reception, so we spent a long time going through suiting and various fabrics; he tried on several, and I tried not to peek at his flat stomach and powerful chest through the gap I swear he left intentionally in the changing-suite curtain. Eventually we found a suit he liked – and looked very good in – and then we chose together a crisp pink shirt, a silk tie and good cuff links. We were both pleased with our efforts, even though it had taken me over an hour to sell one outfit!

As I began to escort the customer to the till, he stopped walking and took my arm.

'You will let me thank you properly, no?'

'Oh, no need for that!' I replied brightly. 'It was a pleasure. I'm glad we found something you like.'

'No,' he said firmly. 'I will take you for coffee. I would like to.'

I smiled. Sometimes this happened. In London once, a sweet old woman, pleased by my service, had left with her purchases only to return fifteen minutes later with a big, sticky Danish pastry for me. Somewhat odd, but most welcome!

'Really,' I said, 'it's my job. Besides, I can't leave the shop floor!'

I was being polite, but was sorely tempted. For one, a coffee was a very welcome idea. For another, I liked the man; I liked the way he smelled, and he had the type of charisma only Continental men seem to have; a way of carrying himself that made him interesting – alluring – to me in a way I couldn't put my finger on. He was not much older than me necessarily – not yet thirty, I didn't think – yet he had the confidence of a much more mature man, and a lovely twinkle in his eye.

'Maybe on my break?' I ventured. 'I stop for twenty minutes, at eleven.'

He smiled charmingly. 'We can have an espresso. It will be my pleasure. There is a café I like three doors down from your shop over here' – he gestured to the right – 'I think you will like it.'

I turned away to allow myself a big grin. I liked the thrill, the newness of the cities, the people I met. The sense of possibility. Going out with Johnny for so long had made me forget just how good it feels to make that initial contact: to make a date for coffee or to see a man naked for the first time; newness is in itself a true pleasure that long relationships can never offer, despite some of their other compensations.

At eleven, I pulled on my jacket and stepped the few yards outside the shop to find my customer waiting for me just inside a quaint old café, with two espressos in glasses.

'What's your name?' I asked, taking my seat opposite him. 'I ought to know the names of strange men I meet in shops and cafés, don't you think?'

'My name is Claudio,' he said. 'I don't need to know yours, unless you're dying to tell me.'

I looked at him closely, trying to work out whether he was trying to be funny, or was just ill-mannered. He was smiling, but he looked serious.

'It's Eleanor,' I said.

'Eleanor. Lovely. Eleanor.' He leaned in to me closely. 'You have only twenty minutes, yes?'

'Yes,' I replied. Oh no. I hoped he wasn't going to suggest anything crass. 'Eighteen, now, actually.'

'OK. Then I don't have time for niceties. I just

wanted to tell you, Eleanor, I think you are a beautiful woman. I have being thinking filthy thoughts about you for the last hour. I wanted to tell you about them.'

I eyed him suspiciously, even though I was flattered. He was silly, overly dramatic, but I still liked hearing his phrases. I noticed a ring on his wedding finger and his eyes followed mine to his hand.

'I am married, of course. I don't think that's relevant at the moment. I just wanted to take you for a coffee and tell you I think you're lovely.'

'You think I'm lovely.'

'Yes. I don't expect anything from you, but I have been imagining what it must be like to touch you, reach inside your little shop-girl outfit . . . I have been having a lovely couple of hours.' He had the grace to look sheepish, and I found I was smiling at him.

'Claudio! What would your wife say?'

'I doubt she would be thrilled. But I assume she meets men, occasionally, that she would like to sleep with. I would rather she didn't tell me about it, but I assume she fucks many men in her mind's eye.'

It seemed a fair point. I was distracted anyway, by the idea of Claudio reaching inside my 'little shop-girl outfit'. His hands were clean and large, the palms turned upward as he spoke. He looked at his watch.

'Fifteen minutes. OK. Come here . . .'

Claudio drew me close across the table and whispered in my ear. His words poured into my head, smooth and silky and filthy. He just wanted me to know, he assured me. There was no agenda. He just wanted to share with me how I had made him feel; what I had made him imagine.

But, of course, in sharing what he had imagined of us, he also made me imagine us. Clever, clever Claudio. I wonder what he is doing now? Eleven minutes, nine minutes, six minutes left of my break, and I squirmed and blushed in my chair as he outlined different scenarios to me. 'I could have touched you in the shop,' he muttered. 'I could have slid my hand inside your shirt and no one would have known. I could have rolled your nipple and stroked your breast and tickled the skin on your tummy. When we were in the changing room, I could have pulled you in. I would have liked to slide your skirt up your legs, have you rub your hand on the tip of my cock' – I was wet now – 'and then I could have bent you over the little chair in that suite, filled you up, fucked you all the way to the hilt, one, two, three, I think you would have liked it, Eleanor, am I wrong?'

His words were quiet, so quiet, but they echoed and rang in my head. I was vaguely aware that my eyes were shut, my thighs parted just a little, and I was rocking gently in my seat. He had me. I opened my eyes. Out of minutes. Back to work.

As if.

'Let's go,' he said, and got up to scoot a few coins over to the desk. I let him take my hand and lead me out of the little café in the direction of my shop.

'There?' he asked, pointing to the shop entrance. 'Or here?'

I looked to where he indicated. A little side alley ran next to the MV store, scattered with boxes and some unwanted bits of furniture and junk. It smelled of old fruit and deliveries, sweet and funky.

I took a deep breath. 'Here,' I said.

Claudio smiled, a big, genuine smile that made his eyes crinkle and twinkle. 'Good,' he said simply, and we walked a few more steps into the alley. We came to a doorway and Claudio pushed me into it and began kissing me deeply. My knees buckled with sudden pleasure but Claudio held me up, powerful and masculine, the scent of him on me suddenly as his mouth covered my mouth, then my neck. My shirt and bra were pulled roughly aside and his warm lips covered first one, then the other nipple. I heard the sound of a buckle and the slide of a belt, and my stomach fluttered. I reached forward to pull up his soft jumper, and feel the warmth of his chest, and he let me stroke his hard body for a few moments before shaking me off.

'Turn round,' he said quietly. I was disappointed – I was enjoying the feel of his skin, and the way he was brushing my super-sensitive breasts with his fingertips, his tongue – but I did not want to break the spell, so I did as he asked.

Almost immediately I felt Claudio grasp at my skirt and pull it up by a few inches, just as he had described to me not long before. My legs were bare, and he pulled my knickers aside and rubbed his hot, hard cock against the backs of my thighs and bottom. I lurched forward and held on to the solid wood of the door in front of me, praying no one would want to use it. The tip of him felt wet on my skin. He pulled back for a moment, one hand on my back still, and I saw from the corner of my eye as he put his fingers to his mouth and then rubbed himself with his saliva. I didn't want to break the spell, but I made myself ask him to use something, and resentfully he pulled out a little silver square from his back pocket, keeping me waiting as he rolled the condom on. I opened my legs a little wider and bent forward slightly, already eager after all that verbal foreplay to feel him slide up inside me.

He pulled my knickers aside once more and fumbled behind me. I felt an odd sensation and then a sharp, sudden pain. 'Claudio?' I cried out stupidly, and then I understood. My pussy was wet and aching and his cock nudged hugely at my arse for a long moment, before stretching me more than I could believe and inching up, up into me in a place I had never been entered before. I tried to say something, but I could not speak, and once Claudio had pushed himself deep into my arse he clutched me tightly again, curling round to kiss me on the mouth and taking hold of my breast to squeeze and rub me again.

There was no pain, exactly, but it felt like nothing I had ever experienced before. I felt every slow movement deep, uncomfortably deep, inside of me. My nipples were alive, but my cunt ached with disappointment and I felt overwhelmed and out of control – deliciously so. Claudio's moans in my ear were sexy but it was frustrating, being toyed with, humiliated in this alleyway – an alleyway! – my pussy wet but ignored.

His groans grew louder in my ear, his thrusts firmer and more impatient. 'Touch me,' I said desperately, and thankfully he understood. Hoisting my skirt up a few more inches at the front, Claudio pushed one hand down the front of my panties, holding me tightly and bracing us both against the doorway with the other. He never broke his rhythm. As he touched my clit for the first time, I groaned aloud in absolute relief, thrusting back now at him and not even noticing the discomfort; the movements only intensifying the sensation in my cunt now that he was rubbing my clit roughly and quickly. I thought of nothing, experiencing pure feeling and I came as he did, loudly and without inhibition in the cool autumn air.

CHAPTER 7

MADRID

Madrid feels so much more Spanish than Barcelona: everyone says it, but it's true. The proper tapas bars are easier to find, for a start, full of old men and young people alike, throwing their rubbish haphazardly on to the sawdust floors. It was October, and the nights were coming in faster; on my first evening there the air felt crisp and cool after the warmth of the day.

I was learning in my job, and I was also feeling strangely inspired by it. At first, working at MV had felt . . . great, but also the end of the world. Leaving college was so hard. I went from four years of indulging all the ideas about art and fashion my brain could invent, to a 45-hour week that was all about upholding and building on a structured company image. I missed making art. It was hard to accept that my job was so rigid; the transition was so extreme. There was no need to write long dissertations or research garment history any more, both of which facts were a blessing. But I missed creating work for the sake of it: just to see what something looked like. The boxes of photos of willing college friends as my fashion guinea pigs, the collages and videos I'd made for end-of-year shows, all were already collecting dust in my parents' loft in the country. Sam, my closest friend at the shop in London, understood best of all. She was the same age as me, and had come the year before from a graphic design and fashion degree in Manchester straight to MV on a placement that turned into a job. You couldn't ask for more: working for a top fashion retailer within a year of graduating was the dream, achieved by few. Loads of the girls on my course had gone off to work for cheap High Street chains and were still there, waiting for their till work to translate into something more demanding. Others, full of good intentions and entrepreneurial verve, had tried to set up their own labels, but the lack of financial backing and expertise made this very hard. I had dreams of starting my own label in the future too, but wanted to get a good few years of experience behind me first, and I think Sam had similar plans.

Still, even though the job was the right thing in terms of my career, it was just not – that awful word again – creative. But as I said, I found it inspiring. What I mean is, it helped me to have something fixed and rigid for set hours every day, every week. It made clear where my free time was, and how much of it I had in which to think, photograph and draw. While so much overseas travel complicated this split a bit, it also showed me new sights and perspectives. I was spoiled, but at least I knew it.

In Madrid I explored the parks. The city's gorgeous, ancient buildings lined the old streets and peppered open spaces, and I took my camera with me everywhere. I took pictures of people, mainly; people wearing crazy outfits, old women in endless fur, kids in formal, double-breasted coats and boots. But I also enjoyed the light, in the mornings before work and the evenings after, and photographed odd things I'd never been interested in before; curling leaves, and abandoned rubbish. Anything that looked different, or beautiful.

Some people I asked outright if they would mind being in my picture. Francesca was one of those people. The light was caught between afternoon and evening, soft and dimming; the huge Parque del Buen Retiro looked lovelier than ever. I had just taken a few shots of a couple kissing and agreed to email them a copy, when Francesca walked into view with her blue-black Spanish locks and bright blue eyes. I snapped her straight away, before I caught myself and got up to ask for her permission and her name for my records.

She was wearing a bright yellow coat that clung to her tiny waist, and hot pink tights. She looked kind of ridiculous but brilliant at the same time, like a fragile tropical bird. She smiled at my halting Spanish but agreed to pose for a few pictures for me. '*Por que no*?' she replied. Why not indeed?

The camera loved her: the way she looked and moved. Her wide smile and those blue, blue eyes looked lovely through the lens: she was bursting with life and exuberance, almost intimidatingly so, and this came across in the photos – I saw so right away when I checked the pictures for light on my digital camera. She twirled and beamed, and flirted and chatted, and by the time I'd taken thirty-odd photographs of her, I was utterly in her thrall.

It was an odd feeling. Since Teeya, I hadn't thought much about the question of my sexuality. There had been other women in the private club in New York, and I had been turned on by the sight of them, but that had been part of a bigger erotic context. Much of the strange pleasure of that night had come from watching the hypnotic way the men ruled over them – us – making the women true sexual objects in a way that was liberating, I guessed, only because it was temporary; for fun, for role play.

Since Teeya, in fact, I realized I had been exploring my relationships with men in more and more extreme ways. I had let first Daniel and then Claudio take control of my body and pleasure in a way that was new to me and aroused me, but I also saw that this was partly a reaction to what had happened with Teeya. I was testing myself, pushing myself. Maybe I was scared, and wanted to 'prove' that I was straight, whatever that means. Watching Francesca, I knew that ideas of fixed sexuality were no use to me now. If I desired somebody, it was nothing to do with their gender, or their age; or rather it was not dictated by strict ideas about these things. It was not for me to say who appealed to me: I could only recognize it for what it was when it happened, and decide whether to act upon desire or not. I knew that I wanted Francesca now, was infatuated by the look of her and her happy, inviting aura. There was every chance that she would reject me, but I decided that I had learned enough about how to recognize and trust my own wants. I would stop testing myself, and just go ahead and let – make – something happen with Francesca. I just wasn't sure quite how.

'Thank you!' I called out from behind the lens. 'These are lovely pictures. You want me to send some to you?'

Francesca smiled and shook her head no, and made to leave the Retiro. I walked up to her, racking my brain for something to ask, to get her into proper conversation.

'Do you live here?' was all I could come up with.

'Yes.' She smiled again. She really was lovely. 'Seven years. I come from the north, but I prefer it in the middle.' She meant Madrid, I supposed; Central Puerta del Sol, the stone slab in the square at the heart of the city, was bang in the centre of the whole country. 'Do you work in Madrid?'

I explained how I was working for MV in the city just for a few days before going back to London. She asked me where I'd been; had I taken pictures of the buildings and people here or there, the opera, the royal palace? Every part of every city had its own character, I knew that, and I had been slowly making my way around Madrid trying to familiarize myself with the different *barrios* or districts. Suddenly I only wanted to keep Francesca in my sights.

'Whereabouts do you live?' I asked her.

'Near all the shops in the little boutique area. It's very expensive! Very small place.' Her expression grew serious. 'If you don't know people here, would you like to come out with us tonight? I have some lovely single men friends,' she said. My heart sank a little – she had no idea – but the thought of going out with her that night appealed, absolutely. And who knew, if she wasn't interested, maybe one of her friends would turn out to be the thing after all.

I met her in a bar in the gay *barrio*. It was the youngest, most modern district in what was, after all, quite a traditional city. I entered the bar and saw Francesca right off, her beautiful hair brushed out silkily around her shoulders, still in her yellow coat. Bars in Spain could be cold at first, as people didn't seem to believe in central heating, and then as the night wore on and places filled up they would become hot with bodies. Francesca was surrounded by friends and exuded the same sense of fun I had enjoyed about her earlier on. She noticed me and squeezed closer to the person next to her, making a gap for me and pouring me a glass of cava from a jug on the table.

I didn't shift from Francesca's side all night. When the tiny bar was packed full, some of her friends got up to dance.

'Don't you like dancing?' I asked.

'I want to stay here with you,' she said, and though taken aback, I was as thrilled and excited as a t eenager. I touched the side of her face, then kissed her gently on the mouth and felt her tongue touch my lips, and I was lost. Midnight came and went, and two o'clock, and eventually Francesca's friends began trickling away towards cabs and studio apartments nearby. We left the bar and stood outside in the cold, and I took her hand.

'Where's your place?' I asked hopefully. I felt drunk, and happy, and a little bit sleepy, but definitely didn't want to go home on my own.

Francesca hesitated. 'I'll show you. Like I said, it's small, but . . .'

She wasn't joking. Her flat was cosy and colourful, though, with rugs and posters covering every available surface. I took it all in, but I didn't want to give either of us time to think. I remembered what I liked best with new partners – when they delighted me with their enthusiasm for me and for my body – and I resolved through the cava not to hold back. I ran my hands up and down Francesca's small frame, enjoying the feel of her curves, and pulling her top up over her head to reveal bouncy, rounded breasts peeping over the top of a floral bra. I reached behind her, hurried and hungry, and popped the clasp so that I could see and touch her properly.

'I haven't done this for a long time,' Francesca said unexpectedly.

'With a woman?' I asked, stopping to look into her eyes.

'Never with a woman. I haven't done anything intimate for months,' she explained, suddenly shy.

'Why not?' I asked, genuinely perplexed. She could never have been short of offers.

'Just . . . busy with work. You know. And actually, I haven't really liked anybody. I had a boyfriend, but he finished with me in the spring.'

My heart went out to her. Poor girl. Maybe she was still nursing a broken heart. I wondered if I should pull back, in case she wasn't really ready: I was already nervous knowing that this would be her first girl-girl experience and I felt under pressure to make sure she enjoyed it, my cava rush falling away. I hugged Francesca, her narrow topless frame exciting me again.

'Come on,' I said, kissing her hair. 'I'll make us a drink.' We moved together to the kitchenette and she picked up two small glasses and found some ice, and I poured us some icy dry fino sherry from the fridge. I slammed mine back and poured another, patting for Francesca to hop up and sit on the kitchen unit beside where I stood. With the sherry singing in my ears and numbing my emotions for a moment, I decided to treat the opportunity as a challenge. I would perform, in the same way that a man performs: I would seduce. I moved to stand between Francesca's thighs in their tight jeans, and kissed her alcohol-soaked mouth. Her breasts were still bare and cool, and I encouraged her to raise herself up while I struggled with her jeans and tugged them down her legs to the floor. Her bottom naked on the work surface, I stood again between her legs and looked around for something to tease her with.

Reaching for my glass, I took a swig and held one of the ice cubes between my lips, rubbing it then against Francesca's nipple. She yelped with the cold, and I moved down her body, rolling the ice over her flat stomach. I parted her thighs and manoeuvred myself only slightly awkwardly, pushing with my tongue until the ice cube sat buried inside the entrance of her pussy. With my face between her legs I breathed in her scent: she was excited, the warmth of her cunt beginning to melt the ice so that water ran out of her. I was still fully dressed and found the contrast a pleasure, but Francesca's breath was coming faster and she began to tug my jumper over my head. I raised my arms so that she could pull at my T-shirt too, and then I was in my vest and she reached in and touched my breasts, softly at first, running the back of her hand and then her palm experimentally across them, then curiosity getting the better of her, she took both breasts in her hands, cupping them tightly.

'Are you OK with this?' I asked her teasingly. She mumbled assent, and I reached down to where the ice cube had melted, stroked her pussy gently and then brought my fingertips up to her mouth for her to suck her own juices. 'I thought you might be,' I said. 'What about if I do this?'

I moved my fingers down again and rubbed them between Francesca's legs, more slowly this time, and without letting up. She opened her thighs wider and closed her eyes, groaning with pleasure. I felt full of wanton pleasure just to touch her. My own pussy felt hot and impatient under my jeans, but I made myself wait. Looking around the room, I could see a makeshift toy within my reach; I leaned over without moving my hand from Francesca's pussy and grabbed a banana from the fruit bowl, licking its skin a little to help it slide before pushing it slowly into Francesca. I moved it slowly inside her just a few times, all the while playing with her clit, before she began bucking towards me, leaning her head back and moaning and coming and making me smile delightedly with pride and pleasure.

Afterwards she was embarrassed when she saw the banana. I laughed it off and she smiled a little sheepishly; there was no denying she had enjoyed it. I reached out my arms and lifted her from the worktop, and she leaned on me as I led her to her bed.

I must have really liked Francesca, because when she fell asleep within moments of me lying her back on the mattress I didn't resent it, but sat on the bed beside her for almost an hour, stroking her hair and face, before pulling my top back on and letting myself quietly out of her little apartment and her life.

CHAPTER 8

MILAN

Johnny. On my second trip of the year to Italy, I felt a nostalgia and longing for Johnny stronger than any I had experienced since we had split up. The fashion season was in full swing and the pace at work was frenetic, but despite this I felt determined to see some of Milan. In some of the other cities I'd visited I had barely even seen any of the streets in daylight, and this was my last trip of the year, so I wanted to make time to explore a little. But queuing for an exhibition in my lunch break, I saw a striking stone sculpture, unmistakably by the same artist as sculptures I had seen the year before on a weekend trip to Florence with Johnny, and suddenly I was back there with him, giggling on his arm, breathing in his scent and enjoying the feel of his muscles under his skin. Any excuse to touch him back then; we'd been together for ages but I had not then begun to take for granted small pleasures about being with him.

The sudden flash of memory unsettled me. I enjoyed the art show, and returned to work for the afternoon, but couldn't shake off the thoughts that had begun to be churned up earlier in the day. Back at the hotel, I distracted myself with a hot bath, a fluffy towel and a romantic comedy. Enjoying the corny movie, the way the storyline tried to manipulate you up and down, making you laugh and then cry just because it could, I forgot myself and began to relax properly. When the film ended I felt restless and cast around the room for other entertainment; I didn't feel like going out and thankfully had a break in the schedule of after-work shows and drinks.

Inevitably I began channel-hopping, and inevitably the choice consisted of all sorts of even worse films, some soft-porn channels, and some pay-per-view options with blacked-out sections of faces and bodies. I poured myself a gin and tonic from the mini-bar and decided to award myself in this, my final hotel of the year, the proper cliché of hotel porn. I thought it might make me laugh. Or, if I am honest, I wanted it to make me laugh, but I thought in reality it might just make me depressed. And at first, once I'd punched in the right code and settled down to watch a blonde girl moaning at random and talking in a disjointed voice, it was depressing. But then the scene ended, or the little story that had been playing out, and another storyline opened up. It was an odd echo of my day: a red-haired girl in a black beret stood outside an art gallery, looking at the queue and clearly wondering whether to bother, until eventually – looking at her watch – she decided to try to evade the queue and get into the gallery another way.

I watched as the girl on the screen found a back door to the building and slipped through, only to find herself turning a corner and walking smack into a security guard. Not any ordinary security guard, of course: this one was young and blond, blessed with taut muscles (obvious under his beige trousers and shirt) and sea-blue eyes. I expected them to be fucking within moments, but the film ran on innocently, the singsong Italian accents lending a kind of poetry to the cheesy setting and interaction.

Inevitably, though, the redhead and the buff blond began to kiss – I forget how this started – and he was soon caressing her openly over her clothes. I watched as he ran his hands over her black dress and skimmed over her breasts, and there was real pleasure in their groans. She had her hands in his hair and was kissing him passionately, unhurriedly but deeply, and I began to feel aroused even though this seemed to me to be the slowest, most unporn-like porn I had ever seen, in my admittedly limited experience. I shifted farther back on the bed, propping myself up on a vast nest of soft pillows, feeling very aware of my nudity under my gown.

On the screen the couple were still kissing, but now you could see that the security guard was getting hornier. His breathing was louder and he had a different look on his face – his eyes had taken on the glassy, hungry look of true lust. As I watched, the red-haired girl began to unbutton his shirt, revealing the muscular body suggested by his clothes, and stroked his bare chest in wonder. Unable to control himself or hold back longer, the man took her lead and reached inside her wrap dress, feeling his way into her bra to touch her breasts. Her eyes closed and she gasped in pleasure, unselfconsciously pushing her chest out so that she could feel more of his hand.

I was enjoying the lazy pace of the story, even though I was surprised by it, but a shot of the gallery the couple were in reminded me again of the sculpture outside the exhibition earlier that day, and so of Johnny, and Florence. I rationalized with myself for a few minutes but then, in that split-second way that can only seem logical when it comes to lonely nights and ex-partners, decided that it was not only sensible but plain friendly to call Johnny and see how he was getting on. It had been months now since we had spoken, after our last disastrous conversation while we were attempting to transform our relationship from girlfriend-and-boyfriend to just friends. He might not be in, I reasoned, or if he was he might not want to speak to me, but then again he might – and before I was really ready I was dialling the number, half an eye still on the porn film.

'Hello?'

His voice was so sweetly, sadly comforting; familiar and yet lost to me for so many months. I gulped back a sudden, overwhelming urge to sob.

'Hi, Johnny, how are you? It's Eleanor . . .'

A moment's silence.

'Eleanor? Wow . . . I'm good, I'm good. How, what are you up to? It's late, no?'

I hadn't realized. Snug in the cocoon of my warm room and my soft hotel dressing gown, lost in the film, I'd paid no attention to the time.

'Johnny, sorry, I didn't realize . . . is it too late? I'm in a hotel, I'm in Milan, I didn't think –'

'It's fine.' He coughed. 'It's nice to hear your voice again.'

'Yours too.'

'I've missed you.'

I was surprised he said that. Touched, but surprised.

'Have you been drinking?' I teased.

'Yes. Someone's leaving do. What are you up to?'

I blushed. 'Nothing much. Just watching films, relaxing tonight. Just thought I'd see how you were . . .'

'Is this a booty call?' Johnny sniggered. For the first time I heard the whisky in his voice. It didn't annoy me – he was fun when he was tipsy, and I used to like the smell of the whisky he drank. I could almost breathe it in now, the memory was so powerful in my head.

'No!'

'But you're watching porn, right?'

'Johnny!'

'I'll take that as a yes. What else are you going to do in a hotel room?'

'Point taken.'

'Any good?'

'What?'

'The porn!'

I looked at the screen. The couple had moved on from kissing and fumbling with shirts. She was laying on her back on a table and he was poised between her thighs, looking longingly between them. It was sexy.

'I guess it is, actually.'

'In what way? What's happening?'

'Johnny! I rang to see how you were!'

'I'm fine. I'm tired, I'm in bed, I'm a bit drunk. So what's happening?'

'Just . . . there's a couple.' I described the scene, the way they looked.

'What are they doing?'

'Ummm . . . She's on her back on the table, he's licking her.'

'Be more graphic!' Johnny paused. 'He's licking her pussy? Say it!'

'Yes, he's licking her pussy.'

'Is it nice? Is it as pretty as yours?'

I blushed again despite myself. Johnny always used to tell me I had a nice cunt. It made me blush then, too, but I liked it.

'It's nice. It's shaved, pretty much. Bare. So you can see everything.'

'Mmmmm. Can you see his tongue?'

'Yes. You can see him lapping at her. He's good at it . . .'

'Is she writhing?'

'Uh-huh. She keeps arching her back.'

'Does she mean it? Are her eyes closed?'

'Yeah, I think she does mean it. Her eyes are shut, but she keeps opening her legs wider in that way . . .'

'I know that way.' Johnny giggled naughtily, and I felt a lurch in my stomach as I realized that he, too, had probably slept with lots of new people since we had split up. I thought briefly but vividly of the image of his head between a new girl's thighs, licking enthusiastically, sliding and twisting a finger in and out of her as he did so, the same way he knew I liked. I was jealous and horny all at once.

'What now?' Johnny asked. 'Is he going to let her come?'

'No. They're manoeuvring. I think he's turning her over.'

'Ohhh. Yum. Can you see her tits, still?'

'Yes. She's not quite lying flat yet. Her nipples are touching the table but she's raised up a little bit.'

'Is he positioning himself?'

'Yes. Oh!' – my breath caught in my throat; I loved this bit when it happened to me – 'He's just slid in.

Her cheeks are pink.'

'Mmmm. I love that first moment. Is he fucking her properly now?'

'Yes.'

'Is he big? Can you see it moving in and out?'

'Yes. Yes and yes.'

'Hard?'

'Quite. She's moaning, can you hear her?' I held the phone up to the TV.

'Yeah. She seems to like it. You liked it, El, like that. I remember.'

I said nothing. I remembered, too.

'Eleanor . . . are you dressed?'

My heart thumped. I knew what was coming.

'Not much.'

'I miss your body, Eleanor. Will you touch your breasts for me? Say hi?'

'OK.' I reached and pulled the tie on my robe so that it fell open.

'Are you lying on your back?'

'Yes.'

'Stroke your breasts for me. Imagine I'm there. Imagine I'm putting my mouth over one.'

It felt good, and I said so.

'Are you a little bit wet? Can you touch yourself to make your fingertips slippery for me?' I was a lot wet. 'Rub your wet fingers on your nipples. Imagine it's my warm mouth on them.'

'Mmm. You imagine it too,' I said.

'I am.'

'Are you touching yourself?'

'Not yet. I don't trust myself. I'm hard, though. So hard for you . . .'

I groaned at the thought of his lovely cock, feeling so much affection for it. I knew it well; could picture it straining, demanding attention, needing to be sucked.

'What's happening in the film now?' he asked.

I opened my eyes and readjusted the phone receiver, cradled between my neck and ear.

'He's still fucking her. She's on all fours now. She's playing with herself a little bit.'

'Christ. Eleanor . . . I'm so horny for you. Play with yourself a little bit. With your pretty pussy. Have you got anything there with you?'

'Like what?'

'You know. You must have taken your vibe?'

'Yes.'

'Can you grab it?'

'Hold on.' I reached under the bed, and pulled a box out from my suitcase. 'Got it.'

'OK. Put it in your mouth, get it really wet. Then turn it on low, and put it at the entrance to your pussy.'

I did as I was told.

'Tickle yourself. Rub it up and down but don't push it inside yet.'

God, it felt good. I had hardly used the vibrator on my trips and now I couldn't work out why, apart from that I'd been busy. But usually, the more sex you had, the hornier you felt. For now, I was grateful I'd brought it with me. I slid it up and down against my clit, feeling it thrill to the cool, slippery, tingly toy.

'Oh, Eleanor. I can hear you like it. Slide it in now. Push it in all the way. Turn the dial up, too.'

I leaned all the way back, and pressed the vibe deep inside my pussy, just as he asked. I wished he were there to help, to bite my nipples now that all of my body ached for attention, but it was good to hear his voice.

'That's it, Eleanor. I can see you with your legs spread, lying on the bed. I'm there, Eleanor. Can you feel me? My hands are all over your tits. My cock's so hard, and I'm straddling you, sliding your vibe in and out of you, and it's buzzing, and I'm rubbing my cock –'

'Are you?'

'I am now – mmm, I'm rubbing my cock, and I'm shoving this big thing inside you to the same rhythm, hard –'

'Ohh, and I'm rubbing myself too, I really am now –'

'Mmm, do, and I'm fucking you with this thing and your hands are slipping all over your clit and you've spread your legs so wide and they're taut how they are just before you come and your –'

But before he could finish I was coming and coming, moaning into the phone, not knowing anything and only vaguely aware of his calling my name into the phone and groaning himself into my ear across the miles as I orgasmed.

There was a few moments' silence on the line. I imagined Johnny falling back on to his pillow, exhausted, his cock still hard and glistening. I felt a wave of affection for him.

'Are you still there?' I asked.

'Kind of. Sleepy now,' he said. I smiled. The image – the memory, in fact, of post-come moments like these with him, was so vivid to me that my hotel surroundings seemed surreal now that I looked at them. I pictured myself in his bedroom, dropping off in the crook of his big arm instead.

'I'm tired too,' I said.

'It's been really nice speaking to you, Eleanor.'

'You too.' We were polite now, but I meant it. Apart from the obvious reason, it had been really nice to hear his voice and have some familiar sex, even though it was kind of virtual.

'Will you call me again?'

'Yes. I promise!'

'Night, Eleanor'.

'Night, Johnny.' Within moments I was asleep.

CHAPTER 9

LONDON

It was nearly Christmas, when London is at her glamorous, brilliant best. I had taken a week off to relax and to buy and wrap presents, but as the year drew to a close I found myself brooding about the adventures I'd had over the previous nine months.

I had changed so much. Not that I had been so naïve or wholesome before, but I felt that I hadn't really known myself. At work I had been ambitious, hard-working even, but until Paulo offered me my big break I was really just treading water on the shop floor, hoping that my efforts at window dressing, and merchandising whenever I was offered the opportunity, would pay off. Now, I was considered trained and knowledgeable; I understood how the collections worked, season after season, and I understood the way the brand worked and its position in the UK, Europe and across the world. This counted for a lot in the industry and, whether I stayed with MV or not, I couldn't have asked for a better start to my career.

But the real difference in me was all because of the people I'd met and – even though it sounds funny – the people I'd slept with. You can learn a lot from people without talking to them very much. Before I left for Berlin, I'd never had a 'one-night stand' – I'd never had sex with a stranger before. I'd had evenings with male friends that had involved too much wine, or nights out having fun that I didn't want to end, which had resulted in sex on several occasions. But they were different. Safe. It was not so much that I had wanted to experience one-night stands for the sake of it, or that I had a problem with intimacy; I loved feeling loved and adored, and I had never really felt that these emotions had much to do with one-off experiences between men and women. I didn't know then about the kind of simple bliss that can spring up between two strangers, unburdened by the mundane, or even by friendship. Thinking back to that word 'safe', what I had wanted to experience was more of the unknown. I had wanted to take risks – risks in terms of not being entirely in control; of not sticking with what and whom I knew. I had for a long time – maybe two years? – slept exclusively with Johnny. Through most of my time at college I had been faithful to this one man, but by the end of our relationship I had begun to feel that I was missing out. Our sex life had been warm, loving, and enjoyable – Johnny grew to know my body well, and what pleased me, and we really connected. Our phone call had reminded me of that, and I hoped Johnny could remain a friend, and maybe an occasional lover; an important part of my future as well as my past. But, as anyone in a longish-term relationship knows, you make sacrifices for that kind of connection and knowledge.

With Johnny, sex was part of how we communicated our feelings for each other. With many of the adventures I had abroad, sex was more for myself: enjoying the other person, but also just experiencing true sensation, sometimes feeling uncomfortable or uneasy, sometimes having the kind of exhilarating fun you can only have with someone you don't really know, sometimes just concentrating on my own pleasure. Some of the people I had met on my trips had taken me further even than that, showing me more about sex, and the power shifts that lovers can play around with to heighten excitement and pleasure.

This kind of thinking was guaranteed to get me horny but didn't help much with the practicalities of Christmas wrapping and card writing! I sat cross-legged in front of the Christmas tree in my flat, lights sparkling and overpriced candle burning, and got back to the pile of little gifts in front of me. I'd bought treats for all of my colleagues in London. Now that I was back for good – save for the occasional trip – I wanted to bond with them again, and get back into the good books of those who'd felt a little alienated by my absence and my promotion. We were going out that night, to a glamorous new club in the East End, where burlesque dancers and fire-eaters were rumoured to appear after midnight. About fifteen of us were meeting in a bar beforehand, and I couldn't wait.

At nine o'clock I was walking from the tube, dressed up under my coat in my festive finery: a red crepe tube dress with some beautiful wedge heels to match. I had put on a little more weight already in the run-up to Christmas, and the dress showed off my increasingly bouncy breasts perfectly. I loved getting ready for a dressy night out: the rituals of bathing, moisturizing, getting my make-up just right and my hair falling just the way I wanted it. I knew these things didn't matter in the scheme of things, but sometimes it felt so good to spoil myself, especially in my new world where every night out could lead to a new encounter or adventure. The months of welcoming Johnny to my room or flat in my pyjamas were a distant memory – now I never risked going out in unmatched or greying underwear! I liked buying beautiful bras and lacy shorts and knickers, and I liked the little shiver of excitement it gave me – even in changing rooms – imagining who I might meet that would make me want to take them off again. Picturing or remembering these things could get me so hot I couldn't help myself. Only that week, I had been in my favourite lingerie shop – trying on a gorgeous set in black satin that pushed my breasts roundly together and flattened my tummy in a very pleasing way – when I'd had a flash of memory, and suddenly I was in Italy, Claudio pushing my knickers aside and easing his fingers into me. I had dropped to my knees in the changing room, and silently licked my fingertips before edging them into my knickers, re-imagining the sensation of his palms on my buttocks, the feeling of being stretched and him pounding and breathing behind me, filling my body and mind, and I played with myself and came as quietly as I could, my eyes shut, Claudio fading from memory as I struggled to catch my breath. I bought that underwear, funnily enough.

Arriving at the bar that night, I was pleased to see that the others had dressed up too. We teased Karl, one of the men I worked with, for his choice of venue – it was obvious from the beautiful boys behind the bar why he had picked it, and there was a Polish guy in particular that he could not buy drinks from without blushing wildly and trying to ply with Bison Vodka! Lots of the other people in the bar were clearly going on to the burlesque night too. Although it was dark, I could see that many of the girls had really made an effort, swirling their hair into forties pincurls, or fifties ponytails and quiffs, dressing either in pencil skirts and seamed stockings or faux-wholesome prom dresses with lots of cleavage showing. There were lots of groups of boys there too, in cute suits or dapper hats. It was impossible to tell who was gay or straight, or how old anyone was, because the dressing up became a kind of disguise, concealing people's real personalities and selves and allowing everyone to be a bigger, alternative version of who they usually were.

We walked to the club an hour later, already slightly unsteady on our feet. There is something about Christmas that just cries out for the most extravagant drinks, so we'd shared a couple of bottles of champagne and were looking forward to a night of old-fashioned cocktails. The club was dark and welcoming, with little tables set around a central stage; there were girls in tiny costumes who brought us trays of drinks, showing off pert bottoms under their skirts. Karl was oblivious to their charms, but Emma and Harry, who I often worked with in merchandising, were thrilled by their glamour. The place was busy already, and as we chatted and drank it filled up so there was barely any room; strangers brushed past and offered smiles and apologies for squashing us, but each time it was a brilliant opportunity to see people close up. I was in a roomful of glamorous, dressed-up strangers and realized this was what I loved: this was where I felt at home.

The chatter in the club was building to a pitch, when a crashing of cymbals announced the first act, and the lights dimmed all the way to pitch black before rising again into a low spotlight on the stage. Nothing more than a round platform six feet across, the stage was designed to place the performer directly in the centre of the crowd: surrounded on all sides, there was no escape for either the act or the watching audience. At first I could see nothing, and then I watched entranced as the lid opened on a box to the side of the stage, which I had not noticed before, and a very beautiful blonde girl shimmied up from its depths. The crowd whooped in surprise and delight, and she smiled, her glittery mouth setting off high cheekbones and feline eyes. She rose to her full height to reveal long legs (and some lovely silver-sequinned slingbacks!) as she stepped on to the little stage, but her body was hidden behind huge, feathered fans, one in front and one behind her. The music built up and she was dancing, moving gently and sensuously and somehow switching the fans to show . . . nothing, but constantly moving and swaying so that you saw only an elegant collarbone or the curve of a hip. I was mesmerized. The audience clapped and murmured and cheered, men and women's faces delighted, smiling, all revealed in the low gleam from the stage lighting. I had the feeling that we were all joined together in making the moment, performer connecting with the audience and the audience with each other, and I wanted the night to go on and on.

Then the dancer's expression changed, and she looked quite cheeky as she moved a fan across and up to show first of all the curved underside of one pale breast, then the other, then rising to show the full swell of proud breasts topped off with sparkling nipple tassels. I heard Harry beside me gasp quietly as she moved to make the tassels twirl and twist, her breasts shuddering with the effort, and I found it unbearably sexy to watch her and also to watch Harry's lustful expression. I wondered if I put my hand in his lap, would he be hard, would he welcome the intrusion? The club was dark enough still, and all eyes were on the dancer. But before I could fantasize about what might happen next the music was over, the dance was at an end and the blonde disappeared as the lights went up a little and the audience, worked up now, took to the dance floor themselves.

I had seen male strippers and female lap dancers before, and had thought that the burlesque night at the club might be a little bit like that, only with people wearing more fantastic outfits to start with. I had not understood that it was not about stripping, but teasing, and now I had the uncomfortable sensation of having been teased. While the dancer was moving I had made eye contact and thought she was looking at me, and I had wanted to see more and more of her, but she had tricked me and left me wanting more: a true performer. Now I was eager to find the blonde in the crowd; I was turned on. I enjoyed other dances: a buxom woman who ate fire and somehow – terrifyingly – set fire to her own nipple tassels, swinging flames in the tiny confined space and letting them lick up and down her body; and a girl with a real snake, which she rolled up and down her slim thighs and around her waist. But none of the later acts affected me as much as that first one had, and though I had a brilliant night, dancing for hours (and searching the club for her with my eyes), I was frustrated not to see the fan dancer anywhere.

But later, later. The night eventually drew towards its close, and even though it was not quite throwing-out time, Harry had to get up early for work the next day and asked if I wanted to share a cab to north London. As we left the warm, smoky atmosphere and stepped laughing into the cold night air, I bumped into the dancer, struggling to put her coat on as she made her way down the steps. Made bold by rum cocktails and happiness, I called over to her.

'Hello! You were brilliant tonight!' I fawned.

'Thank you very much. Is that your cab?'

I looked to where she was pointing. Harry was leaning into the driver's window, but then turned and gave us the thumbs up. 'Eleanor! He'll take us to Camden for fifteen quid!' he yelled happily.

'Oh, I live near there,' she said. 'Can I share with you?'

And we were off.

We had barely been in the back of the car for a minute when Harry leaned in to kiss me mintily. I was surprised, and then not surprised. I pulled away and he moved down to kiss my neck.

'What's your name?' I asked the girl.

'Heather.' She gave me a little smile. 'What's his?'

'Harry.'

'Harry.' She said it softly, nicely. 'Is he your boyfriend?'

'No, no.' I practically shouted it. 'I don't have a boyfriend. I'm single. Harry . . . I work with Harry.' Harry was planting kisses ever lower down my collarbone, making me shiver with pleasure, and he slipped a hand down the top of my strapless dress. Instead of looking embarrassed, Heather watched, interested. Oblivious to Heather for now, to the driver, to me almost, Harry continued to touch me, his hand sliding around my breast to cup it fully under my dress, and then that was not enough for him and he tugged at the top of my dress to reveal my strapless bra and then my bare nipple. He bent to suck it and Heather moved her eyes to mine. Her gaze and the effect of the rum cocktails, mixed with the sensation in my nipple, made me feel dizzy. She looked more than interested now. She looked horny, and I could hardly breathe with anticipation.

'Whereabouts in Camden?' called the cab driver.

He was thankfully obscured by Heather, and I snapped back to attention to tug my dress up over myself and tell him the street name. My heart was beating fast and I made a split-second decision, speaking quickly.

'My place is nearest. Do you want other stops, or . . . ?'

Harry and Heather looked at me. Heather spoke first.

'This is fine,' she said. 'More than fine,' and smiled, and then we were all tumbling from the cab and Harry thrust some notes at the cabbie and I was fumbling with my keys in the lock, and we were in.

My flatmates had already left for trains and family Christmases, and the apartment was quiet. There were vodka-fuelled yells on the street and the light from the streetlamps spilled in through the open-curtained windows, but the flat was still a haven, the little lights on the tree glittering and sparkling and the floor in the lounge still strewn with glitter and tinsel where I'd left in a hurry earlier that night. I kneeled down to clear away some of the mess, and Harry and Heather came into the room. I noticed they were whispering and holding hands, which unnerved me for a moment until they moved towards me together, laughing and pushing me into a heap on the floor until I was giggling too, mostly with nerves and excitement.

'Hold her arms,' said Harry, and Heather pinned me to the floor. I looked up into her face and she smiled at me sweetly.

'Don't try to move!' she threatened me, 'or I'll tickle you again till you cry.' And she stroked a finger under my arm to show me, which had me squirming immediately, as ticklish as a kid. She pulled me up a little, so my head was propped on her lap – in jeans now, I noticed, rather than feathers! – and I looked down my body to see Harry kneeling between my legs, pulling off my shoes and peeping slyly up my dress. I opened my legs a little wider to tease him, and he grinned.

'What shall we do first?' he asked Heather, trying to seem cool but sounding breathless, with an obvious hard on pressing through the soft material of his trousers.

'You go,' said Heather. 'See what she likes.'

So Harry slid his hands gently up and down my thighs, making me tingle and ache for something harder. 'OK,' he murmured. 'Do you like this?'

'Yes,' I said. 'More.'

'More?' Harry paused, then slid his hands a little higher under my dress, tracing the curve of my bottom above my hold-ups and the edge of my knickers. I squirmed to meet his fingers, growing more aroused with his touch. Heather gently, pointlessly, held my arms above my head, knowing I did not want to be anywhere else.

'More?' he asked again, and he looked at me with the question, and I nodded and lifted myself for him so he could pull my wet knickers down, revealing my pussy to him for the first time. 'Hello,' he said quietly, and bent down to breathe hotly against her.

I closed my eyes with the intensity of the sudden pleasure. Harry had let my dress ride up over my hips and remained kneeling before me, licking me lazily along my inner thigh and tracing tiny patterns with his warm tongue over my pussy, just about grazing her so that I was wild with arousal and frustration. I looked up into Heather's face and she came down to kiss me, gently at first and then responding to my excitement, kissing me harder and exploring my mouth with her tongue as Harry's tongue became more insistent. My head was filled with pleasure and I could not discern one tongue from the other; I felt hands on my bottom and more dainty hands snaking down my dress again on to my breasts, and the feeling in my cunt intensified just as I felt Heather squeeze my breasts and I came, crying out again and again, pushing myself as hard as I could into Harry's face. I lay panting, spent, on the floor, only vaguely aware of Heather and Harry above me.

'Who's next?' asked Harry, impatience obvious in his voice. I looked up to see him unbuckling his trousers, and then levering them down over an impressive bulge in his shorts. He did not wait for an answer. I was exhausted by the power of my orgasm, still trying to take in what had happened, but I watched almost dispassionately as Harry took hold of me and turned me over, expertly rolling on a rubber before bringing me back down on his lap and shoving his cock with indecent haste far up into my sopping pussy.

Even though I had just come, the relief of feeling full and being fucked was huge. Harry's palms were placed firmly on my arse and back, forcing me into a half-kneeling position, so that I was open and at his mercy, facing Heather who was still kneeling before me. Her face was flushed, her lovely mouth plump and pink, and I helped her undo her cashmere cardigan and throw it to one side. She had not bothered to put a bra on but was thankfully tassel-free, her temptingly pert nipples hard and firm. Harry groaned behind me and I knew he could see Heather's breasts, and would be able to see all of me from where he kneeled upright. He fucked me a little harder and I put my arms out to Heather to steady myself, my skin brushing against her nipples. Somehow she managed to reach down and unbutton her jeans, squirming to peel them off and coming back to me naked but for her knickers. I put a hand between her thighs to feel her panties; they were silky and wet. She moaned, and shifted, and lay back to lean against my sofa, spreading her thighs before me as she did so.

I took the hint, and leaned down further, burying my head between her legs and licking gently at her clit. It was hard to concentrate as Harry thrust again and again, showing no sign of letting up, moaning with pleasure to see Heather spread-eagled before him now too, her breasts bare as she reclined while I lapped rhythmically at her cunt. She tasted hot and salty and good and her pussy was bare and neat. My own cunt was starting to ache and I put my hand between my legs, rubbing my own clit now as I licked Heather's, and as she began to groan louder and louder my pleasure began to build. I think Harry enjoyed hearing us as he fucked me still more firmly and began to make telltale noises, getting more and more overwhelmed, and then I forgot both of them, limp in Harry's hands as he pulled me more tightly to him and exploded in my cunt as I made myself lick and lick even as I came, half hearing Heather's cries but full in my head of my own pleasure, coming and coming and full of cock, my mouth full of cunt and my head full of stars, and everything went black for a while.

EPILOGUE

This all seems so long ago now. Only a couple of years have passed, but I wonder where the time has gone, and part of me wishes I could have that time again. I thought I was leading in one direction: I assumed I was restless, and that my secret life was part of a youthful period of experimentation I could just put behind me when I was ready to move on to a more conventional, settled future. But I'm not so sure it's like that.

I don't work at MV any more. Once the new year began, and I realized how much I missed the travel, I couldn't stay with the job. I was still only twenty-four then, and I thought it would be easy for me to throw everything in and take myself and my camera on a trip to some of the places I hadn't been to with work: Thailand, Australia, New Zealand, for a start. And it was easy, but there were people I was more attached to than I had realized.

Daniel, for one, is never far from my thoughts. I've been back to New York a couple of times, and we found some special places to go to when he came to visit me in Paris when I was there last year. But I think that's all we want from each other, and I don't want anything to change or spoil what we have, whatever it is. I'm used to it, too: us being a small part of each other's lives, and not knowing much about what the rest of it is like.

And Paulo. I had told him airily in the office that I was handing in my notice to fly away, and he stared at me and turned pale, and the atmosphere grew heavy as we both realized we were on entirely new ground. I had barely ever seen him show emotion before, and his wan wordlessness was unsettling.

'Where are you going?' he eventually asked. He let me gabble about my plans: the things I wanted to see and my hopes of building a new career around photography as I travelled, while he just listened.

'Little El,' he said. 'It's all my fault, this wander-lust, isn't it?'

I shrugged. I was eternally grateful to him for the world he'd unlocked for me, but now didn't seem the time to tell him so. I looked at him properly for the first time in a long while, and noticed the lines around his eyes and mouth.

'I thought you'd get that all out of your system,' he said. 'I meant to make a move on you, when you were done flying and fucking your way around the globe.' But his smirk was back, he was absolutely in charge of his feelings again, and I did not know now how much he knew, or whether to take what he said at all seriously. Our odd dynamic was back on track after a brief blip; we both knew where we were again, and I was relieved.

Later, Paulo gave me contact details of a few people he knew at travel magazines. In my first months away I managed to get several photos published and even scrape together a few travel articles, and with luck and persistence have managed to start a new career as a travel photojournalist. It's not easy, and there's not much money in it yet, but I'm working on it.

Mainly, though, the work gives me freedom. The kind of freedom to travel where I like, stay as long as I like, and meet who I like. I don't know about settling down any more. Maybe some day. But for now, freedom means everything to me, and I don't want to stop having new experiences, new identities and new lovers as I go from place to place. There's plenty of time to be less selfish, but for now, the only person I love to please is myself.